When a Man Cries

Siphiwo Mahala

UNIVERSITY OF KwaZulu-Natal Press

Published in 2007 by University of KwaZulu-Natal Press
Private Bag X01, Scottsville, 3209
South Africa
Email: books@ukzn.ac.za
Website: www.uknzpress.co.za

ISBN 13: 978-1-86914-131-8

Editor: Andrea Nattrass
Cover designer: Flying Ant Designs
Typesetter: Patricia Comrie

Printed by Pinetown Printers

To my parents Gwebani and Nosingile Mahala, whose remains
nourish the soil of Grahamstown.

Acknowledgements

This book reflects insights I have accumulated over the years through experience, observation and imagination. In this regard I would like to acknowledge everyone I have interacted with and who has influenced my life.

My thanks go to my editor Andrea Nattrass, who spent long hours making sense of the words I had jotted down in writing this story. Parts of the novel have appeared as short stories in various literary journals and anthologies. However, I started writing seriously towards producing a novel while involved in Crossing Borders, a Creative Writing Programme organised by the British Council and Lancaster University, London. In this regard, I would like to express my sincere gratitude to Beth Webb, my mentor in the programme.

I thank Keorapetse Kgositsile and Mbulelo Vizikhungo Mzamane whose infallible wisdom as elders and literary giants illuminated my mind and inspired me to release my creative energy, resulting in this novel.

My gratitude also goes to my sisters Nozuko, Ntombizandile and Siphokazi who are always trying to understand what is on my mind. I am grateful to my wife, Miliswa, and our daughter, Mihlali, for appreciating that as a husband and a father, I am also a creative person.

I could not resist using my father's name, Gwebani, in order to portray some characters as close to reality as possible. I have also used my clan name, AmaMpandla, whose praises I sing. However, apart from reference to certain places, historical incidents and public figures such as Grahamstown, Makana, Nelson Mandela and Chris Hani, this story is purely fictional and any resemblances to reality are coincidental rather than intentional.

But in Grahamstown,
those who know say,
anywhere you go is uphill
From Keorapetse Kgositsile's, 'In the Naming'

1

A strong man

A man who fails to retain his dignity and protect the image of his family is a disgrace to all humanity. I have given my utmost best to hold on to things that make one quintessentially a man. I was circumcised according to the custom of my people and had my foreskin removed without uttering a word in agony. I was man enough to hold back the tears as I watched the charred remains of my parents retrieved from the ashes after their house was engulfed with fire. But today I have betrayed the very manhood that I worked for so diligently. Today I cried.

A man who cries in public not only disgraces himself and his family, he also denigrates the dignity of manhood. I have disgraced my father's name, a man respected by everybody in Sekunjalo even years after his death.

It was here, in this dreadful settlement that my parents lived their last happy years and died. The dog-kennel-like structure in which they lived and the generally pitiable state of life in the settlement are the factors that motivated me to lend my brains to my books and make a life for myself. Today I have a house in the formal part of the township, a feat that my parents could not achieve in their lifetime.

But even with all my success and social prominence, I cannot claim to be fully liberated from the intricacies of Sekunjalo. The settlement consumes you and, before you know it, you embrace its ethos. You do not just become part of it, you become Sekunjalo – at one with those characters who walk its streets, fill its shebeens, churches and hospital, graduate in its schools and become fat-cat business people and politicians – and Sekunjalo becomes you.

The bond that I share with Sekunjalo is further strengthened by the death of my parents, whose ashes litter the soil of Sekunjalo and fertilise its trees. The death of my parents is an excruciating memory that still lingers in my mind. I clearly remember the day they were unceremoniously removed from this Earth.

That night I had had difficulty falling asleep but I finally did. Then I was woken up at four in the morning by a violent knock accompanied by a young man's voice shouting, '*Umlilo e*-Sekunjalo! *Umlilo!*' He repeated the same words like a mad parrot while knocking frantically at my door.

'Where is the fire?' I asked as I jumped from my bed.

'He says it's at Sekunjalo,' my wife, Thuli, explained.

I never asked what business I had with the fire, because I thought of my parents who lived in the squatter camp, or informal settlement as they are called these days. I put on my shorts and opened the door. The young man's eyes seemed about to pop out of their sockets as he explained that Sekunjalo was in flames.

'Let's go!' I said to him, despite the fact that I was still half naked.

I ran like a lunatic possessed, hurrying to see if my parents had survived the flames that had engulfed the squatter camp. The stench of burnt objects assailed me from a distance. By the time I got to the spot where my parents' house was, the fire had already been extinguished. The air was filled with smoke and I realised that part of the smell came from the remains of my parents. The wedding ring on my mother's finger was the only thing that helped to identify their bodies.

As I stood there, looking blankly at the ashes of what were the remains of my parents' bodies, I heard Thuli's sweet voice saying, 'Be strong, honey. You've got to be strong.'

I turned to look at her. Her eyes were overcast with grief and I felt helpless but I tried hard not to show it to her. She flung herself into my arms and for a while we stood there, motionless. I felt like for the second time I was vowing to spend the rest of my life with her. Both my parents had gone and now Thuli and Nozizwe, our daughter, were the only family I had left.

There was no time for crying. There was a funeral to arrange. A funeral of a couple who gave birth to me, a couple I had intended to give a better life to, and a couple I adored so much but never had an opportunity to show how much I cared.

The only way I could show my love for my parents was to give them a decent burial. To do this I was forced to deal with Mabelana, the local undertaker who was infamous for his affection for money. When Mabelana complained that things were not going well he meant that people were not dying in as large a number as he would like to see.

As I knocked at Mabelana's office door, I saw a wide smile spread across his plump face.

'Hey, teacher Limba, how wonderful to see you,' he said, stretching out his right hand to greet me. As we shook hands his felt as warm and soft as a sponge.

'Hey, Mabelana. I wish I could say the same,' I said, indicating the purpose of my visit.

'Come have a seat. Don't tell me you are not happy to see me after such a long time.' Mabelana made a weak effort to force a smile on my face.

'It's not that I'm not happy to see you. It's just that I didn't expect to be here today.' I looked down, my elbows on the table and the palm of my hands cupping my forehead. 'Not for the reason that brings me here now,' I said, releasing a deep sigh.

Each time I had to explain the death of my parents to someone the pain seemed to intensify. I could not tell the tale without reliving the experience.

People's words of sympathy did nothing to ease the pain of losing both my parents at the same time. It was even worse with someone like Mabelana, who thrived on such losses.

'Oh, don't tell me you know someone who died in the fire last night,' Mabelana said, looking at me anxiously.

'I wish I didn't, but yeah. It's like that. Both my parents died in the fire,' I said, covering my eyes with both hands.

'Both of them?' Mabelana said in a high voice, looking at me with astonishment. He gave a big sigh and began to wipe his forehead with his white handkerchief. His appearance suggested he was deeply touched by the death of my parents. He looked even more devastated than I did.

'I saw your parents just last week.' He paused briefly and shook his head. 'They were leaning on each other on their way to the community hall to get their pension grants.'

The pain in me intensified as I sat in front of Mabelana. The conversation was like rubbing salt into the still fresh wound that had been opened by my parents' unceremonious departure. I could visualise the two of them leaning on each other on their way to the hall. What troubled me most was that I had not been available to drive them to the community hall on the day. My preoccupations at work had not even allowed me to visit them the previous weekend.

'Of course, I couldn't talk to them because I was looking for this blind scoundrel who has been avoiding me for the past three months.'

'Mabelana,' I got irritated with his remarks, 'can we talk about the funeral arrangements now? I really don't have much time.' I knew if I was not vigilant Mabelana would have gone on and on telling me about things that did not interest me. Fortunately he seemed to notice my seriousness and agitation.

'Oh, *ja*. I understand, *Meneer*. It's just that I'm deeply moved by your parents' death. I'm really sorry to hear that. I'll make sure that I get you the best coffins for them.' Mabelana instinctively rubbed his hands together like a young man preparing to throw dice. It was said that he always reacted that way at the slightest smell of money.

'You know, my parents always mentioned that they would only be separated by death. It is clear now that even death could not separate them.'

I said this with pride because death is a natural thing. One way or another it will strike. The only way to defeat death is in the manner you succumb to it. A person who dies with integrity is better than someone who lives as a compromised shadow. My parents had achieved this. They died an honourable death and remained together as one through to immortality.

Mabelana took out his handkerchief again and wiped the sweat that was popping out on his bald patch.

'It's extraordinary that I'm going to have a funeral for a husband and wife. It never really happens that way,' he said, as he opened the drawer and took out his 'Big Book'.

The book was where he had a list of affiliates to his funeral scheme. People said that in the same book he had a list of those who were likely to die in the near future, and a list of rich families who could bring business should they lose loved ones. Not too long ago Mabelana had been accused of retrieving a casket for recycling shortly after a funeral in the township. But that was township gossip; I don't normally pay attention to such things. My purpose was to arrange my parents' funeral.

'It's not just that. What's even more amazing is that when their bodies were retrieved from under the ashes, they were still holding each other so tightly that they couldn't be separated. Their bodies had merged into one bundle of human flesh.'

I said this with the intention of convincing Mabelana that the two need not be separated.

'Oh, I'm going to tell my boys to prepare a double site for their coffins so that they can be buried next to one another,' he said.

'No! I don't want it that way. Their bodies are not going to be separated. They are going to be buried in one coffin.' I thought Mabelana had understood my point but seemingly he hadn't, or he didn't share the same viewpoint.

'What? In one coffin! No, *Meneer*, I cannot do that. It is totally against the law. The doctors have to do something to separate them.' Mabelana had raised his voice.

'What law are you talking about, Mabelana?' I was getting agitated as Mabelana continued with his lies.

'According to the rules of the Funeral Administrators' Board of Southern Africa each individual buried has to be paid for. This applies even to women who die while pregnant. We count them as two.'

As Mabelana said these words, I realised he was making up a story to convince me of his standpoint. Mabelana knew I knew he was not telling the truth, but I had no time for arguing about funeral costs. Only one thing ruled Mabelana's world – money. That was the only language he understood and the only thing he cared about. If you wished to discuss anything with Mabelana you had to put money on the table. A good friend to him was the one who brought him money or, at the least, the one who'd give him tips about ways of making money.

I don't usually pay heed to township gossip, but Mabelana seemed to be lending weight to the rumours that he had once travelled up north trying to find a medicine man to provide him with wealth. I failed to understand the logic because, as far as I knew, the medicine man depended on donations from his clients to make a living. Some said that when Mabelana was a toddler he learned to say 'money' before he could say 'Mummy'.

'So this is about the money? Mabelana, I don't care about the money that this funeral might cost. I want to give my parents a decent burial. That's all I need from you. Put my parents to rest in the most decent manner possible,' I said emphatically, without noticing that I had raised my voice. I knew Mabelana would do the impossible for the sake of money. As long as the price was right, if you told Mabelana to stand on his head he would; if you told him to kill a lion with his bare hands he would; if you told him to run around naked he would.

'It's about the law, *Meneer*,' he protested. 'But, because it's you, I can bury them in one coffin if you pay for two.' He finally came out with his motives, which had been all too clear to me from the start.

'It's all right! I'll pay for two coffins although you're going to bury them in one,' I said to cut him short. Whatever Mabelana was trying to say, the bottom line was that he desired more than was due to him. For lack of alternatives, I let him arrange the burial of my parents.

With the help of Mabelana the news about the death of my parents and their funeral arrangements was on the tongue of every township resident. There were many fabricated stories about why I had decided to bury my parents in a single coffin. One version that reached my ears was that I was saving money from the funeral policy so that I could buy myself a new car to replace my rusty 1982 Chevrolet, which now looked more like a wheelbarrow on four wheels. People will always have something to say and I had learned that the best way to deal with that is to ignore them.

Our people have a way of conducting funeral services, and time management does not feature in their vocabulary. Several speakers spoke about my father and most of them repeated the same thing: that he was a 'wonderful man', something we all knew.

Among the speakers was old man Jongilanga, my late father's best friend, who was supposed to talk about my parents' death. Old man Jongilanga was a walking encyclopedia of the history of our people and he knew my father's life story intimately. He began his narration from the moment he had met my father, which was some fifty years previously, and he continued his story despite the fact that more than half of his audience had long fallen asleep.

I felt sorry for those sitting in the front row because they were sprayed with the saliva that shot through the old man's missing front teeth. Our custom dictates that we allow elders to voice everything that is in them, especially at times of bereavement. As if my father's biography was not enough, old man Jongilanga went further to give me morality lessons.

'Son of Gwebani,' he continued, 'your father was a great man. A man of integrity. He gave you the name Themba because he had hope for you and he believed that you would never let his name fade away. It is time for you to prove to Sekunjalo that you will keep your father's good name in this community . . .' Old man Jongilanga continued talking until his vocal chords refused to co-operate any longer.

It was late afternoon when we finally went to the cemetery to lay my parents' remains to rest. As I stood there watching the coffin that carried their bonded remains gradually sinking into the deep hole, I was overwhelmed with regret that I had not had a chance to say goodbye to my parents. I tried to fight back the tears that welled up in my eyes, but I felt hot liquid trickling down my nose.

'You are a strong man, my son. A strong man never cries,' I heard old man Jongilanga saying as he tapped my right shoulder.

2

The making of a man

The spilling of liquid from one's eyes does not necessarily translate into crying. Crying is much deeper than that. It is a sustained expression of unbearable agony as opposed to the flow of tears as an immediate reaction to a shocking incident.

The introspection and retrospection I have suffered through as a man fills me with shame and regret. In all the suffering I have experienced, there is this infinite longing for complete humanness; to have and be all the things that describe ideal human nature. Taking a retrospective view on what made me the man that I am today leaves a deep pain in my heart. At times I find myself wanting to blame my wrong decisions and misguided actions on my upbringing.

I never spent much time with my parents. I was separated from them at the tender age of fourteen when I was sent to live with my maternal uncle's family in Grahamstown. We lived on a farm where the school did not offer anything beyond what is known as Grade Seven these days. An ability to read and write was considered sufficient education for the children of farm labourers. On the advice of my school principal, Miss Lwazi, I was sent to Grahamstown in order to pursue high school education. I lived with my uncle's family while my parents lived and worked on the farm.

Life on the farm was increasingly difficult for my parents. White farmers continued to be killed, and produce, including crops and livestock, was always being stolen. Every black man was a suspect for such deeds.

On one occasion herds of sheep were stolen from the farm where my parents lived. Only one visible footprint was found in the kraal and the farmer believed that no man could have single-handedly controlled the sheep unless he worked on the farm. All of the labourers, including my father, were forced to measure their feet on the footprint. Should any man's foot have fitted the footprint, he would have been charged with theft. Each person stepped on the footprint and moved his foot to increase the print's size. In the end no one's foot matched the print and so the majority of the labourers were forced to make an early exit from the farm.

There are many natives out there who are desperate to get jobs, the farmer argued.

My father was one of the very few men who was not dismissed, but he resigned as a way of pledging solidarity with those whom they believed were unfairly dismissed.

My parents' move into the city was not solitary. They were part of a massive movement of rural dwellers who went to the cities hoping to get better employment after our country was released from the bondage of apartheid. This massive influx of people led to the emergence of informal structures on the outskirts of Sekunjalo Township. This informal settlement became known as the extension of Sekunjalo, to the displeasure of the residents of the formal part of Sekunjalo who did not want to associate with the informal settlement.

My parents became some of the first residents in the settlement. It was meant to be a temporary measure although many have been living there for more than a decade now. They built themselves a two-roomed corrugated iron shack that threatened to collapse at any moment. Each day I was confronted with the reality that my parents lived under very appalling conditions in the squatter camp while I lived with relatives in a five-bedroomed house.

Vusi, my maternal uncle, was a Grahamstown businessman whose lifeless body was found lying cold in a pool of blood next to one of his shops. The corpse had two bullet holes, one in the chest and the other in the back of his head. It was never established whether or not the motive for the murder was robbery as he still had his wallet. My uncle died leaving behind his wife, Aunt Gladys, and his only son, Zakhele.

Some would consider Zakhele to be my cousin, but he is not. Zakhele is my brother. He always will be. He was infuriated by Aunt Gladys's behaviour after the death of Uncle Vusi. Shortly after my uncle's death a man began paying nocturnal visits to Aunt Gladys's bed, my dead uncle's bed.

It was then that I was almost convinced that love is truly blind after all. The man had the thickest lips I had ever seen. His large bloodshot eyes seemed like two red bulbs on his face. He had a scar that ran from above his eye down to his cheek.

Zakhele expressed disapproval of his mother's association with the man, but Aunt Gladys was not prepared to discuss her affairs with him. The climax came when Zakhele asked: 'Mother, what is this man doing in my father's house?'

Aunt Gladys never took kindly to interrogation. Her face frowned instantly and I saw her biting her lower lip. She looked Zakhele straight in the eye and pointed a finger at him.

'His name is Jack, son. Why are you being disrespectful?'

'How can I respect a man who doesn't show some respect for other people?' Zakhele was in a defiant mood. He had once raised his unhappiness about his mother's ways but I never took the situation seriously because I still slept with my tummy full every day.

'Zakhele, you are still a child. I never brought you up to judge older people's behaviour,' Aunt Gladys said emphatically.

'Mother, that man is no elder; I don't know what you see in him. He . . .'

I found myself dropping my fork onto my glass plate with shock and embarrassment.

'Son, this conversation is over! I gave birth to you. You cannot tell me who to go out with!' she said irrefutably. 'I've lost my appetite.' With that she picked up her plate and rushed to the kitchen. After a short while she made a dash to her bedroom and I was knocked back to consciousness by the bang of the bedroom door.

I looked at Zakhele who sat cosily in his chair and continued eating as if nothing had happened.

I did not see Aunt Gladys until the following afternoon when I came back from school. I had not seen Zakhele during the day and I tried to avoid Aunt Gladys because I did not know what explanation I would have given her. It was only after three days that Aunt Gladys started questioning Zakhele's whereabouts. After a week we were getting anxious as no one knew where he had gone. It was a full three months later that I received a letter from Zakhele. It read:

Dear Themba,

I know you must be angry with me that I departed so unceremoniously. At times life demands that a man takes such decisions. I could not stand the humiliation of watching my mother sleeping with another man in my father's bed.

Themba, I hope you understand my frustration; it is not that I say my mother must never be involved in a relationship again. No. She is a young widow and still has life ahead of her. But my brother, it was hardly four months after the death of my father when that man began crawling into my mother's bed. What am I expected to think? Was she so desperate that she could not complete the customary six months of mourning? In my mother's eyes I never saw the pain that is expected from a woman who has lost a husband.

Besides, I don't like the look of the man and the way he conducts himself. My father never drank alcohol and never smoked. That man has the audacity to come into my father's house with a cigarette in his mouth and demand that my mother buy him beer. With whose money? My mother never had a job. She relied on my father's businesses, many of which have now closed down.

I don't wish to transfer my frustrations to you. I just want you to know that my decision to leave the place that I previously called home was a well considered one.

Living in Johannesburg has taught me that you have to enjoy life while it lasts. You live for yourself here. This is a place for strong men, not for softies. Here we thrive at the loss of another man; we live in a world where wickedness is rewarded and kindness is punishable; a world where lies set you free and truth lands you in trouble.

I have decided to build my own kingdom here. Perhaps the reason why my parents called me Zakhele was to encourage me to build life the way that I want it. By the way, no one knows that name here in Jozi. Zakes is my name.

I am telling you all this because you are the only relative I recognise. My brother, my only family, that's what you are.

Always,
Zakes

Reading this letter was in many ways an eye opener for me. I was reassured that my brother was still alive and I had an idea of where he was, even though I did not know Johannesburg. I had also got to understand my brother's point of view. But all of this did not appease the grim reality of living under the same roof as a woman who had lost a husband and been deserted by a son.

Aunt Gladys had no one but me to share her problems with and her problems became my problems. I later realised that Jack, Aunt Gladys's acquaintance, was actually one of her major problems. The man was obviously not too fond of peace. He was a gold digger who always threatened to turn to violence when Aunt Gladys seemed reluctant to comply. For this reason, I had to make sure that I gave Aunt Gladys all the support she needed.

One Saturday evening Aunt Gladys asked me to accompany her to a friend's party. I am not the biggest of partygoers but I went to keep Aunt Gladys company. The room was full of old women, most of whom had eroded teeth and hid their eyes behind spectacles. I took refuge in a corner and killed time with a bottle of wine. As I sat there my eyes darted from one place to another, searching for a prospective acquaintance.

I was not the type to fall for older women, but there was something about one of Aunt Gladys's friends. She could not resist taking cautious glances at me whenever she thought I was not looking. Our eyes met and she smiled, exposing a gap in her front teeth, and winked at me. Not knowing how to react, I released a pressed giggle and shook my head gently.

I took another sip of my wine and looked at her again. She was not particularly beautiful but refusing the overtures of a woman is a reprehensible act to any man. After a few glasses I could feel my head spinning and before I knew it I was on the dance floor with the woman, moving to the tunes of Billy Ocean's 'Lover Boy'.

It was at that moment that Aunt Gladys pulled me by the hand and I knew she did not approve of my liquor-induced affection. Aunt Gladys flung her arms over my shoulders. I instinctively put mine around her waist and we began to dance as if nobody was watching.

I can't recall all the things that happened that night but I remember that when I opened my eyes it was morning. When I tried to lift my unbearably throbbing head it felt like a big stone had been placed on it. I was naked and I was in a big and extraordinarily comfortable bed. I tried to recapture the events of the previous night but they only reappeared as vague snippets. I could recall drinking and dancing, and drinking again.

I got a sudden strong and almost suffocating smell of fried eggs and bacon, which made me want to vomit. While I was still figuring out what had happened, Aunt Gladys appeared with a tray of food.

'Hey, there you are. I thought you'd never wake up. You had too much to drink last night,' Aunt Gladys said, with the most genuine smile I had ever seen on her face. She sat carelessly next to me exposing her yellow thighs which, I must admit, looked pretty solid for a woman of her age.

'Yes,' I said absentmindedly.

'Please try to eat, darling,' she said, and kissed me full on the mouth, thus confirming my suspicions about the events of the previous night. Then she disappeared into the bathroom.

I remained in the bed, asking myself questions but never finding any answers. I was hungry but eating seemed to be the most difficult thing to do. I swore at that moment never to come close to a bottle of alcohol again.

'You still haven't eaten? The food must be cold by now,' the silence was disturbed by Aunt Gladys who had apparently finished taking a bath.

'Do you want me to warm it for you?' she continued with her rather exaggerated hospitality.

'No, I don't feel like eating anything,' I said, wishing she would just disappear and I could erase everything that had happened the previous night.

'Hangover is killing you, heh?' she said, untying the knot of her bathrobe and taking it off. She wore nothing underneath and I was embarrassed to see my aunt's V-shaped pubic hair. She got into the bed beside me and I froze as her breasts touched my naked skin under the blankets. I turned to face in the opposite direction and muttered something like, 'Yes, I feel oozy.'

I was filled with disdain. Her nakedness sent shivers down my spine but she did not seem to see anything strange in all of this.

'Don't worry, you'll be all right,' she said, and began touching my body.

15

I knew she yearned for her conjugal rights, which I had supposedly rendered voluntarily the previous night. Now, however, I had returned to my senses and was not prepared to commit such an unsavoury act with my aunt again.

'Aunt Gladys, how can we do this?' I asked, expressing my objection to her overtures.

'You were so good last night,' she whispered in my ear as she moved on top of me. The fresh combination of body lotion and deodorant, which normally smelt nice, only filled me with nausea.

'Aunt Gladys, you are my uncle's widow, and you have a man!'

That seemed to work because as soon as I uttered these words she stopped what she was doing and sat up in the bed, turning her back to me. She began to whimper softly, covering her face with both hands.

I was bewildered as I did not know Aunt Gladys to be the fragile type. There is something about me and tears. I always avoid shedding tears and I cannot stand watching somebody else cry, especially a woman.

Filled with sympathy I wrapped my arms around her and drew her closer to me. I kissed her softly on the neck. She turned and flung herself into my arms. We were locked in a tight embrace for what seemed like eternity. After a while she lifted her head and began to speak in a very strange and shaky voice with tears flowing freely from her now red eyes.

'Themba, I need you. I need you to get me away from that man,' she said, crying.

'Which man is that?' I was somewhat lost.

'Jack. I don't like him; I never liked him. He is the one who killed Vusi.'

'Aunt Gladys, are you all right?' I wanted to be sure that she was in her right mind before taking what she was saying seriously.

She continued talking as if she had not heard my question. 'That man lied. He said Vusi was having an affair with another woman. I paid Jack to teach Vusi a lesson. And he killed Vusi because he says he was being defiant. You see him here because he threatened to reveal the truth if I didn't sleep with

him. That's why you see me with him. I don't like him; I never liked him.'
Aunt Gladys spoke non-stop like a radio that had been left playing to no
audience.

She burst into more tears and began sobbing like a newly bereaved woman.
I knew only one way to console a woman – by holding her in my arms and,
when the situation demanded, giving her a passionate kiss.

I held Aunt Gladys in my arms while she was crying. I kissed her on the
forehead. She lifted her head and looked at me. I could feel her fresh breath
very close to my nose. She looked me straight in the eyes without blinking.
Suddenly I froze and my mind switched off. I saw only a vulnerable, beautiful
woman in need of support. My hands touched a soft skin, my body temperature
rose rapidly and my member hardened. In a moment of collective hysteria
we embarked on a passionate tongue-wrestling episode. Our bodies rolled in
the comfortable bed and I found myself on top of her. In a few moments I was
huffing and groaning on top of my aunt. She was wailing with ecstasy and
shouting things that I could not make up. Her hands were running all over my
sweating body and her yellow legs were flying in the air. At the point when I
could not control the rhythm of my body any longer she held my buttocks so
tightly that I could barely move. The release of my manly fluids sent me into
blank oblivion . . .

After a while I woke up naked next to my aunt who was comfortably
resting her head on my chest. The recollection of our latest encounter weighed
down on my conscience and I started regretting my abominable action, which
I had committed with my eyes wide open this time.

My aunt had given me pleasures of her underwaist bliss that were far
beyond my imagination. I had committed one of the worst sins that any
nephew could even think of – devouring the sacred territory that belonged to
my dead uncle. I looked at my naked aunt who was sleeping comfortably. I
watched her supple breasts rising and falling with her rhythmic breathing.
Then there was a long explosion from her anus – rumbling like a thunderstorm.
What a great sign of comfort, I said to myself.

Aunt Gladys was definitely pleased with her achievement but I could not forgive myself for indulging in such an inconceivable sin. The knowledge of having devoured from my dead uncle's dish was eating me up. Each time I closed my eyes, wishing that the thought would go away, I would see my uncle's face smiling at me.

How could I have betrayed my uncle, a man who would have given his life for me?

The thought of my uncle informed my next move. I gently pushed Aunt Gladys's head away from my chest and onto the pillow. I looked at her wrinkled face and was assured that she was fast asleep. Her make-up-free face gave her age away, but clearly that was the least of her worries because she had gotten what she wanted from me.

I slowly got up, careful not to wake Aunt Gladys who was snoring the morning away. I looked for my underwear but couldn't find it in the bed. Then I saw my shoes, socks, jeans and underwear, seemingly abandoned the previous night in a pile on the floor. I hastily put my clothes on, tiptoed towards the bedroom door and carefully closed it behind me. I jetted out of the house, leaving a naked woman in bed. I did not know where I was going, but I knew my freedom was not in that house.

3

To be a man

E ven though no one was chasing me I found myself running as I got out of the house. I could hear dogs barking and some seemed to come close to bite me as I ran down Ncame Street. I felt like the dogs were laughing at me as I madly raced along on a quiet Sunday morning.

I certainly did not harbour any ambitions to be turned into a sex slave by my licentious aunt. My knowledge of the conspiracy around the killing of Uncle Vusi further validated my impulse to flee Aunt Gladys's place.

After running blindly I realised I was heading towards my parents' place in the informal part of Sekunjalo. It always happened like that. Whenever I was in trouble my mother was always the first person who came to my mind. She was the one person I was sure would listen to and feel for me, but I was not sure what to tell her. A man who hides behind his mother's skirts instead of dealing with his demons is a grave embarrassment in our society. I had two options to choose from: either to be a man who keeps his troubles to himself or a boy who turns to the wisdom of elders in times of trouble. I chose the latter.

I did not know what to tell my mother, but I knew for sure that being close to her would make a difference.

I arrived at the wrong time, exactly when the sewerage truck was doing its rounds of changing the toilet buckets. The latrines were cleaned twice a week; Sundays and Wednesdays were the designated days. I walked past buckets placed along the dusty street waiting for the arrival of the sewerage truck. The nasty sight of the brown foam drooling over the rim of each bucket combined with the awful stench that filled the air made me feel nauseous again. I tried to walk briskly ahead, suppressing the urge to hold my nose, for people would have said I thought better of myself. Some of the '*kak* boys', as they were spitefully called behind their backs, were my former schoolmates who, due to a lack of decent jobs, ended up taking care of our waste.

When I got home I found my mother bending over a washing basin placed on a chair. Water splashed in all directions as she zealously washed my father's dirty clothes. When she heard my footsteps drawing closer she lifted her head and almost screamed with excitement when she saw me.

'Oh, here's my baby. I was just thinking about you; how are you doing?' she asked. I felt a little embarrassed to hear her calling a man of my age a 'baby'.

'Woman, you are gonna spoil this boy rotten. You still treat him like a baby even though he is old enough to have a wife now,' my father said as he came out of the house holding a portable radio to his ear. It was difficult to get reception in the gorges of Sekunjalo and my father loved listening to radio news and stories.

He usually listened with his good friend old man Jongilanga, and they would retell and analyse the stories to each other once they were over. The most dramatic moments were when there were sports broadcasts on the radio, especially boxing and soccer. Then they would kick an imaginary ball and unleash straight punches and left and right hooks in the air.

'Morning, Father. Morning, Mother,' I greeted. My mother wiped her wet hands on her hips and shook my hand. Father put his hand on my shoulder while holding the radio with the other. He led me into the house with my mother following us.

'Son, why are you visiting us so early in the morning? Is there anything wrong?' father asked even before we could sit down.

'Yes, no, father, nothing very serious.' I could not make up my mind what

I was trying to say. The thing was, Uncle Vusi was my mother's younger brother and I did not want to give my parents a heart attack with my news.

'Knock, knock! Is there anyone at home?' A tall frail man with white eyebrows and a bald patch came to my rescue while I was still trying to figure out how and where to begin my story. How should I tell the story of my uncle's conspired death without mentioning the intimate way in which I had sympathised with Aunt Gladys, which had subsequently induced the truth from her about how my uncle was murdered?

'We are all awake. Come in, come in, Jongilanga,' my father said, welcoming his old friend.

The two men never tired of telling their boyhood stories each time they met. They always contested, albeit without declaring it so, who was and is still wiser than the other. Despite their constant self-affirming parodies, my father and old man Jongilanga were good friends and no one could come between them, not even their wives.

'Well, it is good to see the young man here today. Keep that up, my son. Never turn your back on your people. Never!'

I must have been dreaming to have thought that the arrival of old man Jongilanga was my salvation. In fact, it was clearly a transition from bad to worse – from interrogation by my parents to incessant morality lessons from old man Jongilanga.

'Themba's mother, could you please make tea for my age-mate?' It was a tradition that my mother had to make tea each time they had a visitor. Even though old man Jongilanga seemed more like part of the family, he was still eligible for tea with every visit.

For his part, Jongilanga could not refuse the offer. It is highly offensive to refuse an offer from a good neighbour. To accept something from a good neighbour is to welcome them into your life and cherish them as a good compatriot.

My mother filled the kettle with water even though she had been told to prepare tea only for old man Jongilanga. There was an empty cup on the table which suggested to me that my father had already had some tea that morning. He was going to have another cup just for the sake of kindness. I always wondered what he would do when he got twenty visitors, one after another. The trouble was that my mother always had to wait for my father and the visitor to finish drinking before she could serve herself. My parents only had two cups in the house, which made it impossible to serve tea for everyone at the same time.

My mother pumped the primus stove and used the pricker to make sure that paraffin came out from the valve. She took a match from the cupboard drawer and lit the primus stove. While my mother was busy preparing tea I started narrating my story to the two men who listened with great zeal, nodding constantly but not interrupting. When I finished they simultaneously heaved a deep sigh.

'I see, my son, I see,' my father said.

'Who else have you told about this, son?' old man Jongilanga asked. We all spoke in low voices so that my mother would not hear what the matter was about.

'No one, old man, no one. I ran straight here after hearing the news about Aunt Gladys's involvement in the death of Uncle Vusi,' I explained, even though I could not understand what that had to do with anything.

'Who is that? Who was involved in the killing of my brother?' my mother asked nervously.

I knew that was the beginning of trouble. My father had deliberately let me narrate the story while my mother was preoccupied with making tea. He always emphasised that I must be mindful of my mother's fragile heart, especially when dealing with matters related to her blood relatives. In fact, he had impressed upon me from an early age that I must always treat a woman with the sensitivity of handling an egg, though she is more precious than a diamond.

'No, we are just . . . we are just talking about the various probabilities surrounding my in-law's death. Nothing specific.' My father tried to evade my mother's question.

'Themba, my son, what happened? Who killed my brother?' My mother was getting emotional and there was no way out other than to tell her what had happened. I glanced at my father who nodded, gesturing at me to go ahead and repeat what we had just discussed. Old man Jongilanga still had his hand over his mouth, shocked by what I had told them. I cleared my throat and tried to summarise the story.

'Mom, the man who is going out with Aunt Gladys now is the one who killed Uncle Vusi. He was hired by Aunt Gladys to . . .'

'Then what are you waiting for? Why don't you tell the police? My brother's killer has been found and all you do sit around here and gossip!' my mother shouted.

'Woman, we are still trying to figure out what to do about this. It is not good to act out of emotions. We must reason before doing anything.' Old man Jongilanga tried to convince my mother of the wisdom of this course of action, but clearly he was wasting his time. I knew my mother as a kind and docile woman, but that day she showed me something else.

'Reason! Did you say we must reason? What is there to reason about, heh? If you are scared to talk to the police just give me your pants!' She spoke in a high voice and had tears in her eyes as if she had just been told that her brother had died.

'Okay, wait, MaDlomo.' My father used my mother's clan name, which he rarely did. Being called by your clan name evokes deep emotions because it connects you with your elders, your forefathers and all your blood relations. My mother immediately went silent, like a blaring radio switched off by a power blackout.

'We need an objective mind on this matter. This is a delicate situation and we must not act out of emotions. Let us hear what my good friend Jongilanga thinks of this situation. Over to you, my friend,' my father said as if he were chairing a formal meeting.

'Thank you, my age-mate. This is indeed a very delicate matter. I think it is proper that we allow Themba to go to the police. I was not there. You were also not there when this woman confessed to Themba. If called upon to testify, we will not be able to state a case of substance because all we are acting on is hearsay. Themba was there. The woman confided in him. Themba should report the matter to the police and let the law take its course. I remain.' After talking old man Jongilanga took his pipe out of his pocket.

'I agree with my age-mate,' my father added. 'Son, go to the police. Tell them what happened. The woman may be arrested and some people may perceive you as a sellout. That is what being a man is all about, son. To be a man also means that you have to stand for the truth, no matter whom it affects.'

'I was always very suspicious of that woman. She must rot in jail. That devil!' my mother said.

I knew how deeply hurt she felt by the fact that she had called Aunt Gladys a devil. My mother was a staunch Christian who always impressed upon me never to judge, wish or say evil about others.

'Okay, Mom, don't worry. I will go to the police station. I will report everything that Aunt Gladys told me,' I explained, hoping that that would fill the void in her.

'She can't kill my brother and inherit everything that he owned. Never!' my mother said irrefutably. I knew I had to go as soon as possible before her emotions overwhelmed her.

I walked hurriedly to the Makana police station, the most decent building in Sekunjalo township. The tall walls, high windows and red bricks were very attractive to passers-by; no wonder almost every resident had spent a night or two in the cells.

When I arrived at the station there was a long queue attended to by a single police officer. The queue was full of people with fresh scars, bruises and black eyes, and the air was filled with the stench of malt. I concluded that many of the complainants had not slept the previous night. The morning's image of my devastated mother gave me the patience to wait in the slow-moving queue.

As I stood there, memories of my uncle began to flow into my mind in torrents. He had driven me to school on the first day of high school in Grahamstown. He used to take Zakhele and me to J.D. Dlepu stadium to sit and watch soccer all day on weekends. How he had loved soccer; he had even bought the local soccer club's full kit, quite against Aunt Gladys's wishes. Uncle Vusi had been a very generous man and he had been quite popular among the ladies as well. I remembered one day when he came to visit us at the farm. I was doing Grade Three and we shared the classroom with the Grade Four class. My Grade Three teacher was Miss Thema, who had something going on with my uncle. Apparently Uncle Vusi did not tell Miss Thema that he was coming to visit, but she noticed his car in our yard and decided to pay him a visit that night – only to find him in bed with Miss Khuzwayo, the Grade Four teacher.

I don't know what happened between the three of them that night, but the following day we had a very strange lesson. Miss Thema was in her favourite red dress and she began the lesson with, 'Class, today we are not going to start with Mathematics as we usually do. Take out your language books because we are gonna do spelling.' We immediately put back our mathematics notebooks and fumbled in our bags to find our language books.

'Please write the following sentence: "She is ugly".' That was not a very difficult one. We wrote the sentence and looked at our teacher. The second sentence was more complex for Grade Three learners, 'She wants to take other people's men.' We looked at Miss Thema with bewilderment.

'Write!' she instructed us as she sensed some hesitation.

Miss Khuzwayo, whose Grade Four class was in the other half of the room, started giving the same lesson. Her first sentence was, 'He does not want her.'

The pace of the lessons picked up and the teachers did not wait for us to finish a sentence before giving us another one to write. The lessons, which had clearly become exchanges between two adversaries, continued until the intervention of the principal who called both teachers to her office.

My mind was still far away when I heard the man behind the counter shouting, 'I said next!'

I jumped forward and mumbled my apologies.

'Yes, boy, what's wrong with you? Did you find your girlfriend with another man last night?' The enormous, loose-limbed, pitch-black police officer was clearly pleased with the fact that he had authority over all of us in the room.

'Morning, sir. I've come . . . I've come here to report something.' I did not know where to start.

'C'mon, speak up boy. Do you think I'm your woman or something?' the man shouted. I did not want to raise my voice because then everyone would know what the purpose of my visit was.

'I know who killed Vusi Mavi.' The words just ejected out of my mouth. I had not meant to be that blunt.

The police officer looked at me quizzically and after a while asked with shock in his voice, 'Who Vusi? The late Vusi Mavi? The famous business man of Makana?'

I nodded.

'Boy, don't joke with me. This is serious business. Mr Mavi was a respected man in this area and we tried to trace his assailants, but clearly they covered their tracks very well.'

'I know who did it. His widow confessed to me that she hired my uncle's killer.'

'Son, this is no laughing matter. Are you serious?'

'I'm very serious, sir.'

'Here, write your statement. Everything! Don't leave out any detail. Next!' he shouted for the next person in the queue while I looked blankly at the clipboard file that he had pushed to me. I had to sign as a complainant and I did not consider myself as one. I was not an informer either. I was just there to share information with the police.

Well, eventually I did write a good three pages but still there were some details that I left out – the details of our passion that very morning were not for public consumption. I read it one more time and was confident that I had written down everything that needed to be said.

The policeman was still busy taking a statement from a loud woman when I pushed the clipboard back to him. He immediately ignored her and went through my statement while the woman went on about the irresponsible father of her children who spent money with his mistresses.

He kept nodding as he read the statement. 'Very good, very good, my son,' he said eventually. 'This is good information. We'll catch them. We'll arrest both of them. I was always suspicious of the association of your aunt with that man but there was no tangible evidence.'

As I walked out of the building on that Sunday morning I was overwhelmed with a feeling of guilt that my aunt, the woman who had looked after me for so many years, the person I had been in the throes of passion with that very morning, was heading for jail because of me. But I found solace in the reality that I had stood for the truth even if it meant my integrity as a man would be questioned.

4

A man must grow

The arrest of my aunt was more detrimental to me than I had imagined. It marked the beginning of my life in the shacks as all the assets she had inherited from my dead uncle were confiscated by the state and the banks, including the house in which we lived. Some of the businesses had already closed down, she owed huge bank loans, and even the house itself was now far behind in payments. I was left with no option but to stay with my parents in their two-roomed corrugated iron shack at Sekunjalo.

Moving back to my parents' house was a setback in many ways. I was used to the high life of having my own bedroom and sleeping in my own bed. I remember the first night that I had a bed to myself at Uncle Vusi's house. I was so excited that I turned it into a trampoline. I had wild visions of myself as a gymnast in the Olympic Games as I jumped up and down on the bed. Now I was forced to sleep on the floor in the same room as my parents. Their bed, which they had slept on for as long as I could remember, squeaked at the slightest movement. I pitied my father who forfeited his conjugal rights on my account. I remember one night when he thought I was sleeping. The bed squeaked despite his calculated and cautious movements as he slowly climbed over my mother. I cleared my throat with the intention of making him realise I was awake and could hear every movement they were making.

'Son!' he called out to me.

'Dad,' I responded, trying hard to repress laughter.

'Are you awake?' I knew he wanted to ask why I was awake.

'Yes, Dad,' I duly answered.

'I see,' he said, and heaved a deep sigh that expressed nothing but disillusionment. With that, another night went by without them savouring the pleasures of underwaist bliss. On my side, it was another tranquil and pleasant night free of the panting and groaning of an elderly couple.

My parents' predicament due to the lack of privacy in our house was nothing compared to the misery I had to go through as a young man living in this township. You see, growing up in Sekunjalo taught me that survival in a township takes its own form. There are certain unwritten rules that every resident must adhere to. If you dare to disobey the rules you suffer the consequences. Once I unknowingly disobeyed one of these rules and the scar at the back of my head bears testimony to that occasion.

It was embarrassing because Thuli, my girlfriend at the time, was there to bear witness to the horrible incident. It was a cold winter evening and, as a warm-blooded teenager who had just realised that a woman's breasts were not as sharp as horns after all, I was looking forward to a sublime night with the beautiful Thuli at my side. Thuli was a sparkling star in the rather dark and gloomy township of Sekunjalo and she had fallen into my hands. She had caramel-brown skin with a face of rounded cheekbones, big brown eyes, and dimples on both sides. She was slim and tall with firm breasts, a flat stomach and round thighs that would arouse any man. On this night Thuli had made up a story to her parents that she had to sleep over at a friend's place with whom she was to do trigonometry. Her parents, who could neither read nor write, were thrown by the big words that their daughter was using and did not ask any further questions. I had managed to get Thuli out at night but now my problem was that I had no place to lie down and mind lovers' business with her.

I had to find someone who would provide me with a *slaap plek* to sleep with Thuli overnight. I thought of my friend, Sizwe Mfuphi, whose parents were wealthy and generous enough to build their son a separate room in their back yard. Sizwe was a very reasonable fellow who, for his *slaap plek* entrepreneurship, charged nothing more than a nip of brandy to keep him warm through the night. He would only head home when chased away by the shebeen queen, which was usually after midnight. Then he would go into the main house and collapse in his sister's bedroom, which was empty because she was at boarding school.

While on our way to Sizwe's place, Thuli and I passed a group of young men playing dice under a streetlight at the corner of Nompondo and Ncame Streets. I had heard about a notorious group of gangsters called Mongroes, who were famous for their proficiency in using knives with the skill of a butcher. One of them called out to us, '*Heyi, yizan' apha!*'

As I heard his hoarse voice I felt the adrenalin rising in my blood. Thuli wanted to stop but I tightened my hand on her and took a pace forward. The man called out again, '*Ndithi yiman' apho!*', telling us to stop.

I turned to look and saw the tormentor holding what appeared to be a glittering blade. Without another thought I ran like the wind. I could hear the men shouting, calling for others to catch me but no one came any closer. Suddenly something hit me in the back of my head. I stumbled and my lips and chest touched the ground. For a moment the world went blank and then I saw stars making circles in front of me. A stone flew past my head and I realised that the sooner I disappeared the better. I snatched a glance behind me and saw the tormentors closing in. I ran like I used to during my sprinting days, with stones flying behind me, and thumped my exhausted body against the door of Sizwe's room.

'Hey, what's wrong with you? Why did you come in without knocking?' Sizwe asked.

'I'm sorry, man, I . . .'

But even before I could explain Sizwe interjected, 'My goodness! You've got blood all over your back. What the hell happened to you?'

It was only then that I felt the sharp pain and the blood on the back of my head. My upper lip was becoming numb and I could taste a bitter liquid in my mouth.

'I . . . I got in a fight with about ten Mongroes,' I explained.

'You got in a fight with who?' he asked with disbelief.

'With the Mongroes,' I said, proud that he would understand that I could take a stand against the notorious gang.

'You must be joking. No one fights with those guys. Mongroes don't fight – they kill,' he said emphatically.

'I . . . I sort of fought them. The fellow that got me here came from behind,' I said, pointing at the wound at the back of my head. 'But I managed to snatch the stick out of his hand and beat him up with it.'

I had to be creative otherwise Sizwe would have thought me a weak man.

'Let me get some water to clean the wound. And, by the way, where were you going?'

Now reality hit me. I might have saved my life but I had left Thuli at the mercy of the gang. The Mongroes were also known for making their way into women's underwaists, irrespective of the victims' age. For young girls, according to the creed of the Mongroes, salvation lay in acquiring a companion within the gang.

Thuli arrived as I was about to explain to Sizwe the purpose of my visit. She did not have a single scratch on her.

'Thuli, you made it!' I said.

'Of course, I made it,' she replied, smiling and showing her dimples.

'How . . . I mean . . . did they do anything to you?' I could not hide my bewilderment.

'Nothing happened to me because my brother is a member of the gang,' she said. I sighed with relief as I heard her explanation. 'And why did you run away?' she asked.

'I wasn't running away. I was going to get a stick.'

In the olden days having a scar at the back of your head was a sign of cowardice. That's because in those days men carried sticks wherever they went. As a modern man I did not carry a stick all the time. There was no shame in running to fetch one.

I realised that my salvation depended on making friends with Thuli's brother and his companions. I developed friendly relationships with the fiercest thugs in the neighbourhood as insurance for my safety and the safety of those close to me. Of course, I had to pay a protection fee by buying them beer whenever they asked for it, which was usually every time I bumped into them.

My nocturnal excursions with Thuli continued without any particular hindrances because of the protection fee I paid to Thuli's brother and his gang. The problem came when Thuli told me that she suspected something was wrong with her body.

'Something like what?' I asked.

'I'm getting fat and I've missed my periods,' she said in a low voice, frowning.

'You've done what?' I was exasperated. I knew what it meant to miss periods and I was definitely not in a position to raise a child.

'I think I'm pregnant,' she said, blinking several times in an attempt to hold back her tears.

'Thuli, you are joking, right?' my mouth was saying.

'I'm serious, Themba,' she said, now sobbing.

What frustrated me the most was that we were both finishing high school and dreaming about going to the same university. Thuli wanted to be a social worker while I wanted to do any degree that would find me a job. I had never been the fussy type; any job would do for me as long as I got paid at the end of the day.

'So, who did it?' It was not that I ever suspected Thuli of seeing another man. I was just so alarmed to hear that she was pregnant. It had never crossed my mind that our nocturnal excursions could produce a two-legged creature.

'What do you think you were doing? It is not just water that you were releasing!'

'I'm sorry Thuli, I'm just . . . I just want to know how far it is now?' I had to think on my feet.

'Four months,' she responded.

'Four months? So, when is the baby due?'

'I guess around about May next year.'

'Damn, Thuli! That means you won't be able to go to university next year.'

'It's either that or I terminate the pregnancy.'

'What? Terminate it? No ways,' I objected.

'Yes ways, unless you have a better plan.'

'Thuli, I'll marry you as soon as I find myself a job. The little life that's growing in you could be a foundation for our family.'

'But that's only a plan for the future. How do I deal with the pregnancy now, given that my parents won't accept it?' Thuli's parents were as old fashioned as my grandparents were. They were ferocious disciplinarians whose life principles were rooted in the past and highly influenced by religion. They still considered falling pregnant outside marriage to be a disgrace to the girl and her entire family.

My father had been forced to marry my mother after she fell pregnant. Now history was about to repeat itself. I had gotten a girl pregnant and the pressure to find a job and marry was enormous. In spite of that, we could not both give up our schooling. Thuli came up with the idea that she should go to stay with her relatives in a remote village in the Transkei while I continued with my studies. After the baby was born, Thuli would return to school and pursue her ambitions of becoming a social worker. In return, I had to make a commitment to marry her once I started working.

I only knew from reading Thuli's letters that I was the father of a beautiful girl named Nozizwe. I missed those glorious days of witnessing the birth of my daughter, seeing her growing up, starting to crawl, stand, walk, talk, and all the things that make a man complete as a father. Thuli's family would not let the dog that had bitten their daughter and destroyed her future anywhere close to their village.

I did not see my daughter until four years after she was born when I was eventually reunited with Thuli. This was when I started teaching at Sinethemba High School. I had grown up and qualified as a teacher and now I fulfilled the promise I had made four years earlier – I married Thuli.

5

A boy is coming

We were three years into marriage and still there were no signs of growth in the family. In my culture it is crucial to have children when married and I was getting increasingly worried as there seemed to be no progress in this regard. Normally the blame would have been put squarely on the shoulders of the woman. But everyone knew that Thuli was not barren as she had not experienced any problems in conceiving and giving birth to Nozizwe. Furthermore, our lack of production could be associated with the fact that my parents had only had one child.

When I was growing up I was very curious to know why I did not have any brothers and sisters. My mother always dismissed my questions by saying that they loved me too much and did not want to split their love between me and a sibling.

'But all my friends have elder brothers who fight for them in the streets,' I would motivate.

'You are a very strong boy, my son. You can fight for yourself,' she would argue.

'But I want to have a brother to play with, Mom.' I never gave up without a fight. I stated my case, not worrying about where children came from or what they would eat when they arrived, let alone the attention that they would get from my parents at my expense.

'God of our fathers, what is wrong with this boy?' she would exclaim.

'Nothing wrong, Mom. I just want to have siblings.' I enjoyed seeing that I was frustrating her with my questions. That always made me feel clever, just like an adult.

'Your parents are too poor to buy and raise another child, my son,' she said. I had been told that children were bought in a far away place and brought to the house in a balloon. As I grew older I challenged this myth because other children at school had given me a different explanation, which I now understand to be more accurate.

'But Mom, other . . .'

'Please take the broom and sweep the floor,' my mother interjected before I could argue further.

'But that's a girl's job,' I said, partly because I was too lazy to do the job and partly to emphasise my point about the necessity of having siblings.

'In this house there is no girl's or boy's job. You have to learn to take care of yourself.' I knew to be careful when my mother spoke with that tone of voice. What usually followed was a slap across the face if I persisted with my irritating remarks.

It was only after my parents died that I got a different explanation for my lack of siblings from old man Jongilanga. His version made more sense, but it was not an easy story for him to tell. His response when I first asked him was, 'My son, some things are better not known.' I could tell that he was uneasy about the subject as he was usually very keen to narrate stories, especially about my parents.

'Old man, I was circumcised and made a man according to the custom of my people. There is no kind of pain that I cannot endure,' I said, trying very hard to appear strong and confident.

'My son, I am not the right person to tell you about this. Your parents should have told you before they went to the other world.'

'Old man, if I could bring them back I surely would, but now they are dead and buried. You are the only one who can tell me the truth. Please tell me the whole story.' I could not hide my desperation.

'*Tseh*, my son, this is too difficult for me,' he said, wiping his forehead with his hand.

'I'm listening, old man,' I said, eager to hear what was kept hidden inside the old man's bony chest.

'You see, when your mother fell pregnant, your father was not working.' Old man Jongilanga began his narration as if he was about to tell a story of ancient times.

'Yes, I am aware of that, old man.' My mother had told me this all the time as a way of encouraging me not to leave school before I was finished.

'Your maternal grandfather was a much respected man in this land of Makana. A man of honour. He was known and respected by everybody in the whole region,' Jongilanga said, drawing a circle in the air. 'He was one of very few people in our community who could speak the language of the white man perfectly. Some said he spoke it even better than some white people.' He wiped away the spittle that was gathering at the sides of his mouth.

'Other than the teachers, your grandfather was the only person in this region who wore a tie when he went to work. At first he was a clerk at the post office and later he was employed as a court interpreter.' Jongilanga put emphasis on the word 'interpreter' as if it was the best thing to have happened. Perhaps it was because in those days the position of court interpreter was considered to be one of the most prestigious for a black person. He could sit and have tea with the white judges who would try to solicit information about other black people from him. If they were not in an investigative mood, they would use him as an anthropological subject.

'Yes old man, but I am interested more in my parents than in their parents,' I said, getting irritated.

'That's where I am trying to get to, my son. You see, your mother knew that your grandfather would not take too kindly to her pregnancy. She . . . how do I put this, my son?' he asked, taking a puff from his pipe, which was not lit.

'Put it exactly the way it was, old man. All I'm interested in is the truth,' I said eagerly.

'My son, your mother tried to terminate the pregnancy. But clearly you were a very stubborn fetus. Your strength was recognised even before you were born. You spat the strong herbs of the greatest medicine woman in the region of Makana.'

'So, you're saying my mother tried to abort me?' I found myself asking.

'Circumstances didn't leave her any options, my son. It was a major disgrace for an unmarried girl to have a baby. Besides, your father did not have a job either.'

At times old man Jongilanga sounded like a politician – never giving direct answers. Nevertheless, he revealed the unpleasant truth that my parents did not want me, before I was born at least. I never doubted their love and care for me until they responded to the call of the grave.

'I see. Go on, old man, I am listening,' I said, eager to hear more. I was prepared to hear anything. If news could kill then I would have died the moment I heard I was a survivor of abortion. An illegitimate child. The product of an unplanned pregnancy.

'And, ehm, where is this . . .?' I noticed that old man Jongilanga was nervously fumbling for a match.

'There it is, old man, in your left hand,' I told him.

'Oh, thank you, thank you, my son. You'll understand these things when you grow old,' he said, trying to justify his forgetfulness.

If I live to that age, I said to myself.

'And, eh, as I was saying. When, eh, when the attempted abortion, eh, failed . . .' He took a pause and inhaled deeply from his pipe. He blew smoke through his mouth and nose. 'Your father had to marry your mother and they could not stay in the Makana area. That is how they ended up on the farm where your father got a job.'

'So, I'm the product of careless conception,' I found myself saying.

'My son, you were determined to live and make a difference. Your birth was not just littering the surface of the Earth. That's why we will always have hope in you. You dare not falter,' he said with his usual emphasis.

'Thank you for relating the story, old man. But could this be the only reason why my parents did not have another child?'

'Well, the herbs used during the failed abortion destroyed your mother's womb and she could not conceive any more. You were the first and the last life to come out of her womb.'

Now a similar situation was back to haunt me. I had married Thuli because I had made a promise after getting her pregnant. I had kept my promise and married her and now I was keen to have more children to continue my father's lineage. Nozizwe was growing up fast and I was getting frustrated that Thuli was not conceiving.

Then one Saturday I was out attending a school choir competition. When I got home Thuli was not there and I was not very pleased with that. When she came back she showed no signs of remorse at her absence. I was about to remind her who the man in the house was when she said: 'It looks like there'll be a new member in the family soon.' Her face lit up with excitement.

'What do you mean, Thuli?' My anger immediately disappeared.

'I'm pregnant!' She was almost screaming.

'Are you serious?' It was unbelievable. She had fallen pregnant at the moment when I was busy looking for possible reasons for us not having more children. I wanted to have a child that would be born and grow up in front of my eyes, which had not been the case with Nozizwe, our first-born.

'Yes, look,' she said, taking a small black and white image from her handbag. 'Look, that's the back, and this is the head,' she said, pointing to a white line which ended with a round figure like a knobkerrie. 'Can you see?' she asked.

'Yes, I can see,' I said excitedly. The truth of the matter was that I could not see anything beyond white lines on a black and white piece of paper.

'So, how many months are you now?' I asked, very keen to know when I would become the father of two children.

'He's about sixteen weeks,' she said, with a smile across her face. It was only then that I started noticing the difference in her physique. Her face was plump and yellowish. She had also gained a kilo or two and her breasts had swollen a bit. They were definite signs of pregnancy and I asked myself why I had not noticed earlier.

'You said "he"! So, it's a boy?' I asked excitedly. Having a boy would mean the continuation of my name and my family even after I had ceased to exist.

'That's what the gynaecologist told me; unless it's a girl with three legs. You see that white line between the two legs?'

I was too excited to look for white lines and legs. I grabbed Thuli and kissed her full on the mouth. There is nothing as exciting as the anticipation of a child's arrival among a young couple. My ecstasy at that moment could not be measured. To know that my marriage was to be blessed with a child; to know that there was going to be a boy in the family; to know that my second child, unlike the first one, would grow up in a family environment – something I had really missed in my own upbringing – filled a void in my soul. All of this brought joy to me that words cannot describe unless you have experienced it for yourself.

Well, pregnant Thuli was and a father I became again. But she gave birth to a baby girl. We named her Thembisa, and affectionately called her Thembi.

6

The runaway groom

There is nothing as excruciating as suffering for the sins of another man. My brother Zakes is the kind of a man who never keeps away from trouble. In doing so, he always finds someone else to bear the brunt on his behalf.

The saga started when I wrote a letter to Zakes telling him that I was planning to buy a car after my 1982 Chevrolet had been 'redistributed'. It was becoming increasingly fashionable for young entrepreneurs to redistribute vehicles without the owner's permission. They carried around homemade keys to unlock and drive the cars. My old Chevrolet was actually taken from me at gunpoint. I was given two options: either I let them take my life together with the vehicle or they took the vehicle only. Not surprisingly, I chose the latter.

I was accustomed to consulting with Zakes whenever I needed to make crucial decisions. After all, I trusted his taste. He was the one who had hooked me up with Thuli at high school. He also chose the clothes that I wore when I was *ikrwala*, a new initiate to manhood. I was the best looking *ikrwala* in the township. I had not consulted with him when I bought my first car, and I was worried that had brought me some bad luck. My people's proverb says, 'A man who turns his back on his own people comes to no good end'.

Two weeks passed after I had written to my brother and then one Saturday morning my cell phone rang.

'Hello!' I answered, still half asleep.

'Hey, Themba, how are you man?' a familiar-sounding voice said.

'Who's this?' I asked.

'It's your brother, who do you think? Don't you recognise my voice now?'

It was not that I did not recognise his voice. I was just alarmed to receive a call from him. I had not heard from him in two years. When I wrote a letter to him I was not really optimistic that he would respond. I had heard that my brother lived a nomadic life in Johannesburg, hopping from one place to another. The last time he had called it was because he needed some money.

'Zakes, I can't believe it's you. Did you receive my letter?'

'Of course I did. Listen, don't buy that car. Wait for me. I'll choose the best one for you.'

'Come on Zakes. When will that happen? In another eight years?'

I asked because he had come home only once since he had gone to Jo'burg. He had come to attend my parents' funeral, arriving on the Friday evening and leaving on Sunday morning, offering the excuse that his clients could not cope without him. This time he seemed determined to come home.

'It won't take eight weeks before I get there. I'll spend the December holidays with you. I'm serious, man; I'm coming back home to Grahamstown this December.'

I was especially happy to hear this because Nozizwe had been telling her younger sister about their funny uncle, which made Thembi keen to meet and spend time with Zakes. I knew Thembi would also like him because he was such a good storyteller. They enjoyed stories as long as they could relate to them. My brother was good at storytelling because he injected a little bit of extra spice into every story.

A few days later I got a strange call at four thirty in the morning. It was a woman and she spoke in a language that I recognised as seSotho.

'Hallo! *Ke batla ho bua le* Zakes.'

'Who?'

My seSotho is not that good but I understood that she wanted to speak to Zakes. I was confused because he had not yet arrived in Grahamstown.

44

'Zakes Mavi,' the woman responded in an irritated voice.

'Oh! He . . . he's not here,' I stammered, trying to think of an appropriate answer.

'What do you mean he's not there? He left Jo'burg four days ago saying he was going to visit his home in the Eastern Cape.' The woman spoke like a schoolteacher scolding a troublesome student.

'No!' I tried to cover for my brother. 'I mean he is in town but not in the house right now. Do you wanna leave a message?'

'Yes! Tell him that I had twins and they are boys. They look very much like him.'

'My brother has twins? . . . Hello . . . hello . . .' But she had hung up.

Zakes arrived the next morning. I could not believe my eyes when I saw him. I was like a child seeing presents on Christmas day.

'Hey, big brother, your wife called at four thirty this morning . . .' I delivered the news even before he could sit down.

'Who, my wife? Which one?' he said with astonishment. I was bewildered to hear his questions. I knew my brother was a very generous man when it came to dealings with women, but it had never occurred to me that he would be an unremorseful and public polygamist.

'What kind of a question is that? How many wives have you got?'

'I am not married,' he said assuredly.

'A woman phoned and told me she had given birth to twins and that they look like you. Isn't it great to have boys in the family?'

'That's Lerato. I could tell by the size of her stomach that she was carrying twins,' he said, his face revealing a mixture of excitement and mystification. He was excited about the new arrivals in the family, especially that they were boys. But he later revealed that he was not living with Lerato and that he had other children with different women in Jo'burg. He could not support all of his children on the meagre salary of a mine worker but he helped out when he was able to. I could not understand how my brother managed to be such a cheerful man when he had so many reasons to be dull and gloomy.

The next day we woke up early and left for car dealers in Port Elizabeth. I squeezed myself onto the back seat next to a big man while my brother cozily chatted to a slim girl in the front seat. The journey to Port Elizabeth was not a pleasant one but I took comfort from the fact that I was using a taxi for the last time. The taxi deposited us in the middle of town from where we had to find our own way to the car dealers. We asked for directions a couple of times before reaching our destination. I had never seen so many cars in the same place. The new ones were obviously the most expensive so I had to settle for a second hand car. I was quite fascinated by the way my brother related to the salesman. It was not only that he spoke English so well, but also the way in which he addressed the man as if they were old friends.

We looked around as the salesman showed us all sorts of cars I'd have been glad to have if I had sufficient funds. Then I spotted a silver-grey Toyota Cressida. I knew it was what I really needed and, besides, it fell within my budget. But my brother and the salesman had already passed my choice and were viewing other cars.

'This is the one! Come Zakes, have a look,' I burst out with excitement.

'What? You want that? No, no, no, Themba. You can't buy that. You are still young. Only retired old *toppies* drive those things.'

'But this seems so convenient. It's the right price and my whole family can fit comfortably.'

'What family? You call your wife and two daughters a family? Come let's look around. I'll show you the best car you can get.'

I went with him because I didn't want to argue in front of the salesman. But as we continued our exploration in the showroom my mind was still back at the Cressida.

'This is the one! Hey young brother look at this. This is incredible! This is exactly what you need. It's sporty and very powerful on the road,' Zakes said excitedly.

'You want me to buy this car? Man, this is too small for my family,' I objected as I saw what appeared to be a red shopping basket on wheels.

'That's the good thing about a Golf. It looks small but it's very spacious and comfortable. It takes the same number of passengers as a Cressida,' Zakes explained.

'But look at the price. It's R28 000 and we only have R24 000.'

'It doesn't matter; we'll get it for R22 000.'

'But *Bhuti* . . .'

'Give me the money!'

'What? You want me to give you the money. What do you wanna do with it?'

'Just give me the money!' he said, murmuring between his teeth and taking a quick glance at the salesman out of the corner of his eye. I am not the type to argue in front of a stranger so I gave in. Zakes turned to the salesman who was looking at other cars as if he were seeing them for the first time.

'Well, sir, I think we like this one but it's way too expensive. Look at the mileage. It's been on the road for quite some time.' Zakes spoke softly as if he were not the same man who had spoken so firmly to me a moment before.

'How much have you got?'

'Well, let me count it and we'll see. Can we go to your office?' Zakes suggested.

'Yes, of course. Come this way gentlemen.' The salesman led us to his office and as we got there Zakes opened the bag and spilt the money onto the desk.

'Wait a minute, let me close the door,' the salesman said with excitement as he saw piles of R100 notes bound together by elastic bands. At the moment the salesman turned away Zakes took four piles of R1 000 each and put them in his pocket. The salesman counted what was left, his hands visibly trembling.

'Well gentlemen,' he said, 'you fall short by R8 000. Can't you add at least R6 000 more?'

'No man, we can't afford this car for that amount of money. We can get a similar car for R18 000 at the dealer across the road. You'll have to think about a further discount.'

As Zakes said these words I felt a cold wind of embarrassment running down my back.

'Okay, okay, sir! Now tell me, how much more money can you add to this?'

'Sir, could you please give us a minute to consult?' I interrupted. I could not understand why Zakes was being difficult after the gentleman had given us a R2 000 discount. He was being so kind, he even referred to us as 'sirs'.

'All right, while you go out I'm gonna phone my manager and find out from him how much discount we can give you.'

'Thank you very much, sir. I appreciate your kindness,' I said as we walked out of the office.

'Hey, what are you doing? How can you thank a man even before we get what we want? You are gonna spoil this. Now listen, don't say anything. I'm going to deal with this. We are gonna get this car for R22 000. Period!' my brother emphasised.

'But, what if . . .'

I couldn't finish the sentence; he dragged me back to the office.

'Yes, gentlemen, what have you decided upon?' the salesman asked as we entered.

'Well sir, we want this car and we have been able to get R2 000 more. So we'll take it for R22 000.'

'Okay, okay, R22 000 is fine.'

I was so excited I let my brother keep a thousand rand and I took the other thousand home. I even let Zakes drive back to Grahamstown because he was used to the fast driving in Jo'burg. I was keen to see the excitement on my wife's face when I arrived with a red Golf. I had bought a good car and it was only through the generosity of the salesman that I had got a R6 000 discount. I was grateful for my brother's negotiating skills without which I could not have sealed the deal. I understood that the underlying principle on deals like that was that each party tried to ensure that they were not robbed too much.

I had never been much of an expert on cars but I was sure that the Golf was in a good condition and I did not expect any major surprises.

Even when a traffic officer stopped us on the way home, I was relaxed because I knew my car was in perfect condition. There was no funny sound in the engine, the handbrake and lights were all in order, and so was the car's registration. Then the officer asked for Zakes's driver's licence. My brother got out of the car and after a short conversation I saw him reaching into his pocket. He took out a hundred rand note and gave it to the officer. They shook hands, both smiling, and walked towards the car. Zakes got into the car and tried to start it, but it refused. Perspiration ran down my face as the officer noticed that something was wrong with the car. It occurred to me that perhaps the salesman had not been as generous as I had thought. My brother asked the traffic officer to give us a hand; he pushed the car and Zakes managed to get it started.

As we drove along I asked my brother why he had not brought his licence along. He told me he did not bring it because he did not have one. When I asked him how he drove without a licence he replied that it was not the licence that drives; besides, if he's got money he's got everything. I did not want to spoil the day by discussing my brother and his ways so I just let him drive. To save myself from Thuli's sermons, I decided to keep it a secret that he did not have a driver's licence.

I barely had a chance to drive my car because 'Bra-Zakes', as women called him, always had places to go, faces to see and some business to sort out. I also found myself being his secretary. I received several calls on my phone from different women asking for him. Some asked for 'advocate Limba', some knew him as the 'education inspector from Gauteng province', and others insisted that he was the manager of a certain insurance company based in Jozi, as he fondly called Johannesburg.

I did not understand why Zakes had to tell so many lies; women had admired him and been attracted to him even when we were still at school. I would be desperately looking for a girl but they would always choose Zakes who would use and discard them like old shoes. His motto was 'hurt them before they hurt you'. He had been hurt by Linda, his high school girlfriend, when she fell pregnant by one of our schoolteachers.

Since then, Zakes had never been out with only one woman at a time. His half-truth stories formed a greater part of his charm and he always had some tale to make girls laugh. Of course, now they also admired the broad shoulders he had developed from working with a pick and shovel in the mines.

On one of the very few days when I was driving my car so many women waved at me, calling me 'Bra-Zakes'. I was often tempted to stop and start up a conversation with them, but I was not as versatile as my brother. The only girl I stopped for seemed to be really desperate. She waved frantically for me to stop.

'Hi, can I help you?' I said as she opened the passenger door.

'Where's the owner of the car?' she asked as she sat in the passenger seat.

'I am the owner of the car,' I said, somewhat boastfully.

'C'mon man, don't play games with me. This is Zakes's car,' she said confidently.

'No, this is my car. Zakes is my brother,' I tried to explain.

'Okay, brother-in-law,' she said sarcastically. 'Zakes is my man. Please take me to my grandmother's place at Extension Seven. I'm in a hurry.' She used the word 'please' but it sounded more like an instruction. I drove her there and she got out still under the impression that I was just a chauffeur.

One Wednesday morning during the holidays I got a letter from the principal. She was inviting all staff members and the school governing body to an urgent meeting. She specifically insisted that I should attend the meeting. I was shocked and concerned because we never held meetings during the holidays unless there was something really serious, such as the death of a student or staff member.

Old man Jongilanga, as the chairperson of the school governing body, made one of his long speeches sharing his unending words of wisdom. Eventually he got around to the bad news: 'We announce with sadness that today the community of Sinethemba High School is losing one of its most prosperous daughters. The girl who brought such an honour to this school and respect to the community at large; the girl who has been the fountain of knowledge and a spring of integrity in this school is now leaving this soil of Makana. Miss Phatheka is heading to the city of gold. There is no doubt that this daughter of Phatheka has played a vital role in uplifting our community, which is why I release her with no reservations. Sons and daughters of Makana, may you please join me in applauding a heroine of this community.'

The principal was resigning after fourteen years of service. Miss Phatheka had taught for nine years before being promoted to the position of principal. She was the first female principal in our township and our school had been producing the best Grade Twelve results ever since.

I almost joined the ranks of my ancestors prematurely when I heard the second announcement. The principal herself announced that the school governing board had decided that Mr Limba – that was me! – was to become the acting principal at the start of the following year. After just six years of service at the school I was going to become principal. I, the son of Gwebani, was to become a principal. I pinched myself several times to make sure I was not dreaming.

When I had to make a speech as the new principal I initially did not know what to say. Then the sudden resignation of our long-serving principal faded away and I thanked the governing body for believing in me and entrusting me with such a challenging position. I promised I was going to do my best to ensure that the school maintained the high standards that Miss Phatheka had achieved.

I knew that no matter how hard I worked, I would not be able to improve on what Miss Phatheka had done for the school. She was such an amazing

woman: strict but not abusive, firm but neither stubborn nor aggressive. These
were the reasons why even the male teachers respected her so much.

I couldn't wait to get home and deliver the good news to Thuli. I barely
noticed as I drove through red lights and stop signs. When I got home a
triumphant smile still played at the corners of my mouth. I didn't even wait
for Thuli to ask what the meeting was all about, as she usually did. When I
told her the news, it was one of those moments when she didn't hesitate to
hug and kiss me in front of the children.

As for my brother, when he heard the news he shrugged his shoulders and
smiled. A few minutes later he told me that he was leaving the following
morning. When I asked if he was happy with my promotion, he told me that
he was, but that he had to go. I suddenly realised I would have to account to
many women for his sudden disappearance. Then I asked him, 'Zakes, what
am I supposed to say to all these women when they ask for you? They don't
know who you really are. In fact, I feel like I don't know you myself even
though we are the same blood,' I said, trying to make him feel bad.

'Young brother,' he said, patting my left shoulder with his right hand.

'Just tell my girlfriends that I am what they want me to be. If they want
me to be a lawyer, I become one. If they want to see a rich man in me, I
become one. Dealing with women is quite simple: if you can't convince them
confuse them. That's my mission.'

At first I didn't understand what Zakes meant but I had to take his word
on the matter. Although I did not condone my brother's ways, I soon felt his
absence. I found solace in reading the minutes of the last meeting over and
over again. I can't tell you how many times I read the sentence: 'The meeting
appointed Mr Themba Limba as the Acting Principal of Sinethemba High
School.'

It was during one of those moments of reliving my triumph that I heard a
car hooting outside the house. I went to look and almost fell on my back
when I saw Miss Phatheka's car in the driveway. She came in and asked for
my brother. I knew Zakes had no boundaries when it came to fabricating

stories and I was worried he might have made up a story that I was not aware of. I told her that he had left two days ago.

Miss Phatheka went into instant shock. She was a diabetic and she suddenly began to tremble and sweat popped out on her face. I supported her and made her sit on the sofa while I rushed to the kitchen and brought her some water to drink.

When she regained her composure she told me that she and Zakes were supposed to be getting married and that he was going to take her to Johannesburg to find a better job. She paused for a moment and I sat there not knowing what to say. My sympathy would not have meant much because I had indirectly benefited from my brother's trickery. After a while Miss Phatheka stood up and took her handbag from the sofa. She stared at me with undisguised contempt and then asked, 'Is there any man out there who is honest? You know, in Zakes I thought I had finally found a good man. Why is your brother such a liar?'

Her face was overcast with fury and her voice reverberated with anguish. At that moment I knew I had to be honest with her. If I had made up a story I would have been buying into my brother's school of thought. Truth hurts for a moment but it has the capability to heal wounds that could last for a lifetime.

'My brother turns himself into what women want him to be,' I said promptly.

'Is that the message he told you to give me?' she asked.

'No, it was a message to give to all his girlfriends,' I said. Miss Phatheka stared at me listlessly, sighed, shook her head slightly and made her way towards the door.

7

What awaits a man

That December vacation was a summer of great expectations. I could not wait until the beginning of the new year when I would be the Acting Principal of Sinethemba High School. I would be filling the shoes of the queen disciplinarian, Miss Phatheka. A queen who had found herself in early retirement – thanks to my brother, Zakes.

I think Thuli took this principalship business a little too seriously, to put it mildly. This is one of the things that differentiates my wife's character from mine. I am a laid-back kind of person while Thuli, by contrast, is too hyperactive, if that's the right word to describe her. Maybe not, but she's the exact opposite of me, whatever that is called. Just two days after Christmas day she insisted that we had to go shopping.

'Themba, you are a principal now,' she said, trying to convince me to go with her.

'And so, what does that have to do with anything?'

'You must change your image. You need an entirely new wardrobe.'

'C'mon, Thuli. I'll be working with the same colleagues I've been with for the past six years. What's so different now?'

I tried to argue with her even though I knew it was futile, especially when it came to issues of clothing. I had argued so many times that she had too many pairs of shoes but she kept buying more. It seemed as though each time she had to attend an occasion she had to buy a new dress which had to go with a new pair of shoes, and maybe a handbag as well. I even gave up on buying her gifts after I bought her a necklace and she told me that she had to get earrings to match.

We walked in and out of shops, trying on different suits but not buying anything. Thuli made me turn this way and that, this way and that, just like a model on television. After some close scrutiny she would suggest that we check out the next shop. The reason for not buying would be along the lines of it's not the right label, colour, size, or even that we didn't have the right tie, shirt, or shoes to match the suit. I certainly did not care about all those things. Backwards and forwards we went until I was exhausted.

Eventually I went home clutching three plastic bags containing suits. She promised that we would look for shoes the following week.

'I wear size nine,' I said to her as I retired to bed after the long day of our gruelling shopping spree.

'It's not necessary to tell me; you can try them on and see if they fit you.'

'Nine will always be nine, Thuli. I trust your taste. Please choose for me,' I said wearily. At my age I was not prepared to be turned into a fashion model. Although I had not enjoyed our shopping spree, I must say I fancied the suits that Thuli had chosen for me. I was confident that all the other teachers, especially the female ones, would fancy them too.

I was sure to be a cut above many of the male teachers who never really cared about their image, especially the likes of Sizwe Mfuphi. Yes, that's right, my old friend Sizwe had managed to complete a teacher's diploma from Cape College in Fort Beaufort, and was now my colleague. He was also informally crowned as the king of drunkards in the education sector. The only reason Miss Phatheka had not fired him was that he was a good Agriculture teacher despite his predictable Monday morning sicknesses and emergencies on Friday afternoons.

Of course, Sizwe claimed to be an occasional drinker and he made sure that every day was an occasion. He always found something to celebrate or some frustration to get rid of through drinking. Even sitting with friends was excuse enough to appreciate life by drinking.

At one point Sizwe had a very close shave with Miss Phatheka who caught a boy named Lungile Nkathazo clutching a bottle of wine under his arm during school hours. The boy confessed that the bottle belonged to teacher Sizwe Mfuphi who had asked him to get it from MaDlamini's shebeen, The Ladies' Joint, across the street. It was at our sports day on a Wednesday afternoon that Sizwe demonstrated to his audience of male and female teachers how Miss Phatheka had entered his classroom clutching a bottle of Paarl Perlé wine in one hand and with the other tightly holding the hand of the schoolboy. This is Sizwe's account of what happened.

It was a Monday morning and Sizwe had a throbbing headache after the weekend's heavy drinking. He had to keep the learners busy while he waited for the boy to get back with his 'medicine', and so he sprang a random test on them. He did not have to prepare any questions because the Agriculture textbook came with a list of questions that students had to answer at the end of each lesson. Sizwe, wearing his sunglasses, opened a book in front of him and nodded off to dreamland.

He thought he heard a voice echoing from a distance.

'Mr Mfuphi!'

He lifted his head and the book he was still holding to his face fell on the floor. The learners were standing as a way of showing respect to the principal. Sizwe looked quizzically at the angry principal from under his sunglasses.

'Mr Mfuphi, what's this?'

'Good afternoon, Ma'am. I mean, good morning Miss Phatheka.' He blinked his bleary eyes a couple of times before wiping away the spittle that was drooling out of the side of his mouth. The sight of him dozing off and drooling apparently caused giggles, and later uproarious laughter, amongst the learners – a sound that invited the principal to the class. She was on her way to the class when she came across Lungile, holding a bottle of wine. He claimed that the wine belonged to teacher Mfuphi. Sizwe noticed that the principal was holding a bottle in one hand. The mischievous Agriculture teacher immediately walked towards her wearing a broad smile across his face.

'Oh, thank you, thank you, Miss Phatheka. Did you help him to get it?' he said, stretching out his hand to take the bottle from the principal. The principal let go of the bottle without saying a word. Sizwe turned to speak to the class, holding the bottle in the air. 'What is this, class?' he asked, pointing to the bottle.

'It's wine, sir,' a few students responded reluctantly while others were confused by the strange lesson from their teacher and the presence of the visibly angry principal in their classroom.

'Where does wine come from, class?' he continued.

'Wine comes from fruit, sir.' The class responded in unison this time around. Sizwe glanced at the principal who did not blink as she fixed her gaze on the troubled teacher. He hesitantly looked at the students and pointed at the bottle again.

'And eh, what kind of fruit does wine come from, class?'

'Wine comes from grapes, sir.'

Sizwe paused briefly and asked the students to repeat what they had just said, 'Again!'

'Wine comes from grapes, sir!' The whole class was catching on and responded confidently.

'Very good, sit down!' The learners sat at the instruction from their teacher. Sizwe turned to the principal with a broad smile across his face and nonchalantly said, 'You see, they learn very fast when we give them practical examples. Things that they can see.'

Miss Phatheka shook her head and left the classroom without a word.

Sizwe was later summoned to the principal's office and warned against sending schoolchildren to undesirable places during school hours.

Lungile Nkathazo, whose surname means the troublesome one, was no stranger to being on the wrong side of school rules. At one stage he faced the school disciplinary committee because of his sporadic attendance at school. Lungile was doing Grade Nine for the third consecutive year and his sporadic attendance at school and the homework he was never able to submit were a recipe for another year in the same grade.

I informed Miss Phatheka about my troubles in trying to get Lungile to advance to the next grade the following year. When he showed up at school on a Wednesday afternoon Miss Phatheka decided that we should call him into the office and find out exactly what his problem was. The boy attributed his poor school attendance to his father's ill health.

'My father was very sick. I had to take care of him,' he argued.

'I'm sorry to hear that. Where is he now? Is he in hospital?' Miss Phatheka asked with concern.

'My father is at home; he cannot afford the hospital fees.'

'Oh, then I must visit your father and see if we can do anything to help.'

'No, don't visit my father at home. He is fine now,' the boy said nervously.

'Well, if your father is fine now, why don't you bring him to school? I would like to have a word with him,' Miss Phatheka said, clearly beginning to get suspicious.

The boy came with a man who he introduced as his father. He was tall and had a bony face with tobacco-stained teeth, spirit-damaged lips and uncombed hair. His not so wrinkled skin suggested that he could be younger than he looked.

'Thank you for responding so promptly to my invitation, Mr Nkathazo,' the principal began the meeting. The man nodded constantly as she spoke in a low, sensitive voice. 'We called you here today because your son's attendance at school has not been very impressive. You would know that he is doing the same grade for the third year now, and it is in our interests to see him in the next level in the coming year.' She paused briefly and circumspectly glanced at me. I nodded as a way of encouraging her to relate my concerns about Lungile's performance.

'Mr Limba here,' she said pointing at me, 'has brought it to my attention that your son's attendance at school has been very sporadic, to say the least. We would like to hear from you what the problem is.' Lungile started sweating profusely and his Adam's apple bobbed up and down with nervousness. I got the impression that his father must be a ferocious disciplinarian who did not spare the rod as we did due to the new laws of the education system.

'This son of mine is a very good boy,' the man argued. 'He goes to church every Sunday. He keeps the house clean, and he takes care of me.' As he spoke the stench of liquor filled the room. Lungile's father was not exactly a good role model for his son. I wondered if we were speaking about the same boy because Lungile was definitely not the church-going type. He barely sang any of the hymns we did at school.

'Yes, I hear you, sir. But why is he not doing his schoolwork?' Miss Phatheka inquired. 'You see, he cannot do well at school if he does not attend school regularly.'

Lungile cleared his throat as a way of getting the principal's attention. 'In fact, principal, I . . .' he tried to say something.

'I am not talking to you now boy! Let your father explain what the problem is,' Miss Phatheka interjected while the boy was trying to explain.

'Eh, you see, this boy has been helping me . . .' I saw Miss Phatheka lift her finger as if she had remembered something.

'Excuse me, sir,' she said abruptly, 'what is the name of your son?'

'What?' The man looked startled.

'The name of your son. Who is he?'

'Are you asking me the name of my son?'

Miss Phatheka answered with a nod and looked quizzically at the man. He stared listlessly into space and then turned to the boy. 'What's your name, son? There's just too many of you.'

'I am . . .'

'Shut up!' Miss Phatheka shouted at the boy as he was about to speak. 'What kind of a father does not know his son's name?' It was only now that I began to notice there was absolutely no resemblance between the supposed father and son.

'I forgot to tell you that I am suffering from amnesia.'

'I guess you have also forgotten that this boy is not your son.'

It later turned out that Lungile had grabbed the first man he could find at MaDlamini's shebeen and for the small fee of a half-jack of brandy got him to stand in as his father. His parents were very strict and had no knowledge of the boy's bad attendance at school.

These were the kinds of challenges that I was to deal with from the learners and teachers alike. I wondered if I would be able to tackle them with the same acumen that Miss Phatheka had displayed over the years.

8

A man among men

Being neighbours with the Sekunjalo settlement draws you into the life of its residents. This has both advantages and disadvantages.

The residents of Sekunjalo treated me with affection, like I was a son, and with high esteem because of my role as a school principal. This is the admiration you get when you are a good man in the community.

I later realised that with this respect comes responsibilities and I was obliged to carry out duties that I had never imagined I would do. I found myself having to be the Messiah of the settlement. Every man and his wife came to me with whatever trouble they had, adamant that I could do something to help. This started in a way that utterly hid its potential harm from me. Shortly after the birth of Thembi, my second child, old man Jongilanga and his wife came to visit. They gave us many blessings and wished my family all the best for the future. In turn, I told them not to hesitate to ask for anything.

Now I understand that this was the moment when I set a trap for myself. By opening the door to them I later realised that I had opened it to the whole of Sekunjalo. Old man Jongilanga would come with another neighbour, who would tell me what a good neighbour he had been with my parents. Then they would complain about their living conditions at Sekunjalo. The next day they would come and ask for some water, as they did not have running water in the settlement. I would allow the two men to help themselves, only to find there were four others waiting with their twenty-litre containers outside.

Once I allowed water to the first two, the other four did not need to ask for my permission. They followed the 'give one, give all' policy, at my expense. At first I pretended not to notice the trick they were playing, but the numbers grew even further. I called old man Jongilanga and told him about my anxiety.

'Old man, I have been noticing some unfamiliar faces fetching water from my yard,' I said, cautious not to make accusations or upset the old man in any way.

'Those faces are my neighbours, my son. They also need water.'

'I don't mind when you and your neighbours fetch water here, old man. I am just concerned that their sons might see other things to take from my yard,' I explained.

'I see, my son. I will relate your concern to my neighbours.'

This is one of the things that I liked about the old man. He was not the kind of person who would prolong a conversation just to defend his point of view. He valued anyone's opinion even if it opposed his own.

The number of people coming to my yard did indeed decrease, but the number of containers fetching water never did. Jongilanga would come driving a donkey cart with a friend. There would be twelve or fifteen twenty-litre containers in the cart. I had to be much firmer in telling him that I was not prepared to support the whole of Sekunjalo.

That was not the end of my problems. One night I heard footsteps in my yard followed by the sound of water pouring into a container. I got tired of talking to residents who turned a deaf ear to my complaints so I bought a brand new padlock to lock my gate. But when I woke up the next morning I discovered that the padlock and the gate were gone.

These offences were enough to harden the heart of even the most charitable philanthropist. When I got a notice about an upcoming community meeting I saw it as a chance for me to give the squatter-camp dwellers a piece of my mind.

As far as I understood, I was thirty minutes late for the meeting, but still people were standing in small groups along the corridor. I was filled with anger so I chose not to speak to anyone, lest I should unleash my fury on the wrong person. I sat right at the back in the middle of the row so that I could observe others. The chairperson of the meeting was Skade, the regional Youth League leader and, according to him, a former commander of a section in the Congress's military wing. He began the meeting by welcoming the attendants, especially the 'first timers', as he put it. I knew the specific mention of *first timers* was directed at me.

I had not been seeing eye to eye with Skade and his juvenile remarks were meant to humiliate me in front of the residents. But they did not embarrass me at all because I knew that by the end of the meeting my mission would have been accomplished.

I could not believe that now our relationship was like that of a frog and a snake. Skade and I were once as close as a man and his shadow. We grew up and attended school together. We used to play marbles together and later were on the same soccer team. We had shared almost everything.

Skade's active involvement in politics had sparked the differences between us. How he got involved in politics is a story that still puzzles me. He got arrested in 1985 for a mere public indecency offence. At the time black and white people were not allowed to use the same public toilets. Skade was caught emptying his bladder against a tree and sent for six months behind bars. It was in prison that he met political detainees who recruited him to the movement. When he was finally released it was as a hero who had defied apartheid laws by urinating in public.

Shortly after his release, Skade went to join the military wing in exile. He came back in 1991, after the apartheid government lifted the ban on political organisations. I was already at university, training to be a teacher. Then Skade lost his leg after he was shot during the march to remove the Ciskei dictator in 1992.

Our public spat began when I found Skade telling unbearable lies to unsuspecting and highly impressionable youngsters who were beginning to look up to him as a struggle icon. 'Chris, you know I saved Chris,' he said, beating his chest. 'Those poorly trained homeland soldiers were about to shoot him and I somersaulted and pushed him aside. And they got me here,' he said, pointing to the stump of his leg.

He was referring to what is now known as the Bhisho Massacre, in which twenty-eight marchers and one Ciskei homeland soldier died. It was true that Skade had been one of the many marchers who sustained serious injuries. And yes, Chris Hani and other liberation struggle leaders had been at the march, but Skade never even came close to Chris Hani, let alone saved him.

'S'true's God, I saved Chris,' he said, putting his finger in his mouth and then making the sign of a cross in the air. 'I saved Chris and he wanted me to be his bodyguard . . .'

'C'mon Skade, stop telling lies to my kids. Chris Hani had his own bodyguards.'

'You . . . you don't say anything. You are a traitor. You were busy studying while we went to the forest to fight for your liberation. And you think you know a thing about the struggle?'

I was not interested in proving to Skade that I had contributed to the liberation struggle in my own way. I simply did not want him to distort history and mislead the children who relied on oral narratives to learn about the history of their people. Skade had a tendency to use every possible opportunity to remind people about his prowess as a liberation movement cadre. If he had done something right, it was because he had been trained in Lusaka. If things did not go according to his wishes, it was because people were jealous of him because he had been a freedom fighter.

Skade read out the meeting's agenda, which was composed of issues that did not affect or interest me. But I was determined to stay until we got to the stage of 'Any Other Business', where attendees were allowed to discuss additional matters. The first item on the agenda was the nomination of our Zone's representative on the Makana City Council. Since I was at the meeting, I had to vote, and I was prepared to vote for anybody other than Skade.

The first person to be given the floor to nominate a candidate was old man Jongilanga. Some referred to old man Jongilanga as 'the well of words that never runs dry'. As a young boy I used to visit his house and sometimes spent the night. The family was highly religious and they prayed every night before going to bed, with the old man conducting the sermon. By the time he had finished his wife often had to wake the children who had long fallen asleep during the lengthy prayer. He was the kind of person who would continue speaking even in his sleep. His speeches were not much different. I couldn't understand why Skade had given him the floor first. Old man Jongilanga rose to his feet leaning on his walking stick, which had seen so many years.

'I beg to nominate that son of Gwebani sitting over there,' he said, pointing with his stick in my direction. I was visibly stunned as I had not expected him to get to the point that quickly, let alone anticipated that he would nominate me as a possible representative.

'Gwebani was my age-mate,' he continued. 'The two of us were circumcised together . . .'

'Old man Jongilanga, your circumcision has nothing to do with the current situation. Please . . .' Skade said irritably.

'Young man, don't you dare tell me how to speak. Did you forget to bring your respect with you when you came back from the forest?' The old man had raised his voice.

'What I am saying is that this young man's father was a great man, a man of integrity. He is buried in this soil of Sekunjalo.'

'Old man Jongilanga, all I'm asking is that you please talk about the man in front of us and not about his father. If you have nothing to say about Themba you can sit down and give other residents a chance to nominate candidates,' Skade interjected.

'That's what I'm getting at. You see, that son of Gwebani sitting over there is now a teacher. He is the head teacher of the biggest school in our area. Gwebani's son knows poverty as much as he knows wealth. He knows our ways; he also knows the ways of the white man. He has a very humble background and yet he is such a progressive man. If we want a good leader, we should look for someone who knows how to get his head above the depressing conditions of the township and stand tall as a shining star. Gwebani's son is such a man. I am seated.'

For a moment the room was filled with uneasy silence. It was clear that Jongilanga's words had pierced everybody's heart. It is amazing that as you walk around living your life people are actually observing and analysing you, documenting your actions and behaviour in their minds. I was deeply overwhelmed by the old man's words and Skade was clearly astonished.

'Thank you, thank you, old man,' Skade said with agitation. He continued, 'Now, does anybody agree with what the old man has said? Does anybody want Themba, the man living in the big house across the street, to represent the poor people from the shacks?'

I could hear that Skade had regained his resolve to annihilate my image. I saw several hands immediately dropping like giraffes bending for twigs on a short tree.

'Comrades,' he continued, 'remember that in this meeting we want someone who will represent our needs. We want someone who will stand as our voice in expressing the concerns of the poor and not those of the rich. Now, I say again, does anybody, other than old man Jongilanga, want Themba Limba to be the representative of Zone Six? Please raise your hands right now.'

When Skade finished talking it was so quiet I could hear the heart-beat of a man sitting two rows away from me. For a moment I thought everybody had withdrawn but then I heard a creak from the corner. Another old man, who was from the AmaTshawe clan, stood up and supported old man Jongilanga's view and thus qualified me to contest against whoever else was to be nominated.

'All right, now we need the second candidate. And, remember, we need only one representative and two candidates will contest for this portfolio.'

Several hands went up and I knew immediately that the competition was to be really tough. A young man rose, clutching a red hat with both his hands.

'I nominate you, mister chairperson. I need not motivate my decision because everyone knows your role in the struggle. If it were not for people like you, we wouldn't be here today.' He sat down promptly and more hands rose.

'I stand to second the last speaker. It's about time those who suffered during the struggle are rewarded.'

Contentment was written across Skade's face. I knew he had lectured those boys before coming to the meeting.

'Now, two names have been suggested. From the two candidates, myself and Themba, you will have to choose which man will be your representative. Which man will represent your needs during council meetings; which man will best express the pain and suffering of the poor people of Sekunjalo; which man truly knows what it is to be poor?' He spoke through clenched teeth and placed emphasis on each word.

I was now determined to contest the position to ensure that I did not grant Skade an opportunity to ridicule me and continue with his boasting in the township. The voting began and, to my surprise, I beat Skade by twenty-four votes to sixteen. He could not believe it and asked for a recount, but the results came out reflecting the same margin. He was no longer interested in remaining until the end of the meeting. I was rejuvenated as I watched Skade, filled with anger and disappointment, scurrying away.

9

A man on the move

I took on the responsibility of being a councillor for Sekunjalo with mixed feelings. It was an honour for me to be the leader of my people, but I also knew that leadership had its challenges. Poverty in the whole of Grahamstown was a real and visible thing. The toilets in Sekunjalo were still the bucket system type and the sight of a man carrying a bucket overflowing with human excrement was common in the community. It was the norm to walk past buckets placed along the street waiting for the arrival of the sewerage truck. The majority of the community had no jobs. The few who were lucky enough to find good jobs moved away from the townships to live in the affluent suburbs. I was determined to stay in the township and help lift the scourge of poverty that afflicted the community of Sekunjalo.

Having accepted the responsibility to be a councillor I was prepared to listen to more of old man Jongilanga's speeches. He made another long one schooling me about the morals of leadership.

'Son of Gwebani, you come from the pedigree of a very strong people, the AmaMpandla clan. A house where even a chicken is never defeated; the ones who skinned a leopard alive. We gave you the name Themba because we had hope in you. We still carry that hope and we believe that you will bring salvation to this soil of Makana. We chose you because you are a great man. You have read many books. Your power is in your head and not just in your arms. Your weapon is a pen and not a gun. Your mission is to save lives and not to cause casualties.

'Son of the AmaMpandla clan, go to the authorities. Speak in the white man's tongue. Tell them that we, the people of Sekunjalo, are very poor. Tell them that we live in shacks and that we have no jobs; tell them also that we need water to drink. I take a moment to smoke.'

I found the demands quite pragmatic and very basic. In summing up the long speeches, I highlighted running water and sanitation as the primary needs that required immediate attention in Sekunjalo. Both issues affected me directly. The sight of buckets full of human excrement lined up along the streets was disgusting. Perhaps my parents could have been saved from the fire if there had been running water in the settlement. I was determined to ensure that these basic human rights were granted to the community of Sekunjalo.

The next Thursday I attended the meeting of the Makana City Council on behalf of Sekunjalo. I met Mr Bongani Vabaza, the mayor, for the first time. The man could not have dreamed of becoming a model. He had froglike eyes and his cheeks looked like he was permanently blowing a whistle. He had massive hands and a protruding belly that threatened to break the braces that stretched across it. I still wonder who had advised him to grow his long grey goatee. But BV, as Mr Bongani Vabaza was fondly called, was popular for his eloquence in speech. He was a great philosopher and had a following all over Grahamstown. I was one of BV's fans because of his impressive speeches. He was a product of what practically became the Robben Island College of political knowledge. Many political activists who were opposed to the apartheid government were sent to Robben Island. The intention was to persecute them, but, in stark contrast, many of them came out of prison more politically inclined and educated than ever. BV was part of this generation of politicians and sitting in a meeting with him was an overwhelming experience for me.

What was even more striking was seeing Mr Vabaza's secretary. She reminded me of my wife before her beauty got buried in fat. She had a captivating smile, a face of rounded cheekbones, light skin and brown eyes.

She was adequately endowed with firm breasts like two neat watermelons. I am a married man but I can't restrict my eyes from appreciating the beauty of nature when they see it. It's a problem, I know. Maybe it's not my problem. Perhaps it's a gender problem. A manhood problem, that's probably what it is. Any man who says he never gets attracted to a beautiful woman is a liar. We all do, but most of the time we suppress our feelings.

The beauty that I saw that day was far more deceiving than the snake of Eden. I sat in a strategic position to allow us to make eye contact. An electric current flashed through my body as our eyes met. She dropped her gaze momentarily and then looked at me again. I smiled benevolently. She also smiled. I knew I had made an impact. That's my secret weapon. If I look at a girl and smile in a compassionate way and she smiles back, I count her as mine. I cannot remember the proceedings of the meeting very clearly as my mind was stolen by the pretty sight across the room.

The delegates were ordered to submit their memoranda to the secretary so that the mayoral council could view them. I took this as a good opportunity to introduce myself to her. 'Excuse my prejudice, but I'm sure you are not from around here,' I said to her as a way of starting a conversation.

'Do you know everyone in this town?' she asked without a hint of a smile. I began to wonder if she understood that I was paying her a compliment. She was definitely aware of her beauty and had obviously received many such compliments.

'Maybe not, but I wouldn't forget a face this beautiful once I had seen it.' As I said these words I saw an almost girlish smile playing across her face.

'I bet you are after every beautiful woman in this small town,' she said, still with a smile on her lips.

'Well, I would be if they all looked like you,' I said, happy she was entertaining my remarks. She shrugged her shoulders and released a pressed giggle. I knew right there and then that she would be mine. No woman laughs at my jokes and gets away with it.

'By the way, I'm Themba, Themba Limba, the councillor of Sekunjalo district.' I stretched out my hand to greet her properly. Her hand was as soft as a baby's and I held it for a few seconds while looking straight in her eyes, hoping she would come closer. How I longed to have my lips touching hers. I would also settle for a hug. Not a friendly hug, but one of those tight hugs that leaves no space between bodies.

'Pleased to meet you, Themba. My name is Dolly. I come from Uitenhage.'

'Dolly, what a wonderful name.' I charmed her to ease the tension.

'Thank you!' Her face was beaming with a mixture of shyness and excitement. I decided to let go of her hand, which I had been holding on to all along. The fact that she did not complain or show any signs of irritation further confirmed my impression that she also felt something for me and couldn't resist my advances.

'So, how long have you been working here?' I asked, hoping she would tell me more about herself.

'It's only my second month. I finished a diploma in Office Administration last year,' she said proudly.

'How are you getting home, Dolly?' I asked, hoping she did not own a car.

'I'll take a taxi as I always do,' she said smiling.

'Can I give you a lift?' I offered with excitement.

'I don't think we will be going the same direction. I stay in Section F.'

'That's not a problem. I can take you there,' I said with great confidence.

As we got into the car I was trying to figure out which method I should use to express my feelings for her. It always happens like that. It's easy to tell a girl that I love her when I don't mean it. Words never come easy when I sincerely mean them, not on the first day at least. The silence was interrupted by Dolly.

'So, what do you do, Themba?'

'I'm a school principal.' After a brief pause I decided to add, 'It's a lousy job, I know. But I'm used to it. After a while you enjoy the tricks that teachers and school children play.'

There was silence again in the car. The next time Dolly talked was when she told me where to turn.

'So, when can I visit you?' I asked.

'You can't.'

'How come? Are you staying with a partner?' I asked, hoping to find out if she was seeing someone.

'Not exactly. I'm staying with relatives and they are kind of fussy when it comes to male visitors.'

'Why don't you move into a flat?'

'I'd like to. It's just that I can't afford it at this stage. Maybe in about two months time when I get promoted.'

I was taken aback to hear that she was expecting a promotion so quickly, especially when she didn't have previous working experience to qualify her for a more senior position. I was interested to find out what she had done to deserve promotion, but I could not figure out how to ask without divulging my curiosity.

'Oh, so you are expecting a promotion?'

'Yes, the mayor will create me a director's position in one of the departments in the council,' she said smiling. The issue of a new inexperienced person being elevated to a senior position left me with a number of questions, but I did not want to pursue them now. My mind was on conquering her so that I could be the first to drink from the well of her sexual bliss before the scavengers of Grahamstown could lay their hands on her.

'If I assist you in paying for a flat now, would you allow me to visit?' My experience told me that if she allowed me to pay for her accommodation then ultimately she would become my property. And I would have a smaller house and someone fresh and young to ease my mind when I needed to.

'Well, that can be arranged. But, are you sure . . .'

'Dolly, trust me,' I interjected before she could raise issues about my marital status, which had nothing to do with her. 'Just tell me where you want to stay, and I'll pay for it. Money is not a problem for me.'

'Yeah, but I feel bad about it because . . .'

'Okay, okay, I know as a woman you've got your pride. I like an independent woman too, so I'll pay half of your rent. How is that?' Over the years of my sexual conquests I have mastered the art of channelling the potential partner's mind into my interests without her noticing.

'Let's take things one step at a time. I think you are going too fast . . .'

'Well, I blame that on you. I never fell in love so fast with anyone before.'

I heard a chuckle from her and when I took a glance at her face, I saw her cheeks widening. I knew I had her eating out of my hand. If I had not been driving I would have grabbed and kissed her instantly before she could change her mind. A moment of silence followed in the car. She was probably contemplating the prospects of our imminent relationship while I was busy undressing her in my mind as she sat on the passenger seat. I stole a look at the twins sitting on her chest and my member hardened instantly. I opened the window for fresh air – my blood needed some cooling down.

When we got to Dolly's house I switched off the engine. She unexpectedly gave me a gentle peck on the cheek and thanked me for driving her home. We both got out of the car and walked towards the house. Then we embraced and kissed in the doorway. I walked to the car and before opening the door I turned to look back. She waved and walked into the house. I drove off rejuvenated.

By sunrise the news of our imminent relationship was already flowing in the municipality's streams of gossip. I am only glad that for a while the news remained within the confines of the municipality; I would have been in serious trouble should Thuli have heard about it.

With hindsight, I have a strong suspicion that the news of Dolly and I reached the mayor's big and ever-roving ears. When we convened the following week he was not in a good mood. We were supposed to hear the mayoral council's response to our memoranda, but the mayor's response was, to put it bluntly, that the demands of the people were not going to be met. He told me that if people needed running water and proper sanitation, they would have to pay rent first.

'How do they expect the services to be delivered if they do not want to pay for those services?' he asked.

'The council is looking forward to developing Sekunjalo,' he added. 'Preparations to build a park with a swimming pool are underway.'

'Mr Mayor, I'm sorry to interfere with your plans . . .' I was deeply annoyed but I tried to keep the required level of respect. 'In my view, a park should not be considered as an urgent issue at this juncture . . .'

'Mr Limba,' the mayor interrupted, 'I am disappointed by your shortsightedness. The park is not merely for entertainment as you think. It will help to reduce the rate of crime and disease. One of the major reasons why people commit crime is that they do not have an alternative thing to do. Children from the squatter camp swim in that stinking pool full of maggots across the road. They fill the hospitals because of the diseases that they collect in the dams. The swimming pool will be maintained and kept clean.'

I respected the mayor but I could not let him continue mixing up priorities. 'Mr Mayor, I understand your predicament, but I also understand that, at this very moment, someone in Sekunjalo is living under unhygienic conditions. These maggots you are talking about, sir, are the result of improper housing and sanitation. When the buckets are full, people relieve themselves behind bushes . . .'

'Mr Limba, I'm sorry I have to cut you short there.' I could hear he was getting irritated. 'You seem to be missing the point. We are not here to discuss how and where people relieve themselves. It seems to me that you don't even understand the kind of work we are doing here and, unfortunately, I don't have the time to explain it to you. Just hear me out; it is impossible for any municipality to give free housing to every soul who roams its streets. We do not have accurate statistics of the population of Grahamstown because of people who move in and out of town. Two years ago we asked people to register for free houses in Extension Nine. Do you know what happened?' He looked me straight in the eyes to show he expected an answer. It was clear that he had every desire to humiliate me.

'No, no I don't know, Mr Mayor,' I said with mortification and regret.

'Our people registered for themselves and for their long-lost relatives. We have people who live as far away as Cape Town but own houses in Grahamstown. You know what they do with the houses that we gave them for free? They rent them out. The so-called 'homeless people' suddenly became landlords and landladies. We cannot allow that to happen again. This squatter camp you are talking about is populated with chance-takers from the former Ciskei and Transkei homelands looking for opportunities to get free houses from the municipality.' He took a pause by sipping from his glass of water.

'As I said, Mr Limba, I do not have time to give you all the background. It is for you to find out exactly what is happening around here. Now, let us move forward to more urgent issues on our agenda today. What needs immediate attention is the imposition of tax laws on the street hawkers. We must make sure that all unlawful hawkers are removed from our roadside, especially in the areas of tourist attraction.'

It was clear that the mayor and I had differences of opinion. I did not care what he thought of my questions. After all, anyone could tell I was not his favourite person in that meeting.

'But Mr Mayor, the majority of the population in Grahamstown is unemployed. They survive by engaging in small businesses such as selling crafts, fruit and vegetables. How do we expect them to pay tax under those circumstances?'

I was concerned because I knew what it meant to be a street hawker. As a child I used to sell fruit and vegetables in the streets. The competition was really tough because each and every woman and her children in the township sold the same things. Our target market was the buses that passed through Grahamstown after midnight when the shops were closed.

'If we allow street hawkers not to pay tax, everyone will opt for this so called "small business" and thus avoid paying tax. We cannot subject the municipality to that kind of a situation. No illegal business should be allowed in this city. Everyone must take on the responsibility of paying tax.'

His eloquence did not convince me at all, but I had to compromise as I seemed to be the only councillor who found the situation problematic.

Back in Sekunjalo I had to give a report that would obviously be unacceptable. I tried to impress the community with my oratory skills.

'Elders of the community, fathers and mothers, my brothers and sisters. My fellow residents of Sekunjalo, I greet you in the name of the struggle. You sent this son of Gwebani to represent you in the city council. I took the responsibility with great pride and enthusiasm, conscious of the fact that you entrusted it to me knowing that I am capable and keen to carry it with great determination.'

I went on and on, saying all the things that politicians usually say during meetings of this nature. When I had explained the proceedings of the city council meeting a dark cloud of dissatisfaction settled over the room. Skade was the first person to raise his hand to ask a question.

'Thank you Mr Councillor Limba.' I was not prepared to entertain his sarcasm but had to give him the floor because our democracy guarantees freedom of speech to every fool.

'I must say that I am not surprised by the report you just gave us. It's what I expected from you. I am saying this because I know you very well. We grew up together and, as far as I can recall, you never took on any leadership positions. Not even in the soccer team. It is surprising that some people gave you the responsibility of taking vital decisions for the community when you can't even take decisions for yourself . . .'

'Thank you Skade, your point is noted,' I said with agitation. I knew he had been yearning for my downfall. His remarks did not bother me much though; my obligation was to regain my impeccable reputation in the community. I got embarrassed when old man Jongilanga lifted his hand.

'Son of Gwebani, I stand here as a very unhappy man. If I die today, my soul would not go to Heaven. It would not be welcomed in the ancestral world either. Because my age-mate, your father, my son, would say I let him down by not putting you on the right path.

'Son of Gwebani, allow me to ask: what kind of people did you hold the meeting with? What kind of people would be keen to give water for swimming but refuse to give it for drinking? Son of the AmaMpandla clan, go back to the authorities. Tell them that all that the people of Sekunjalo want are essential services for survival. Tell them that the people of Sekunjalo are too weak to swim. And tell them also that we are too thirsty to play. I remain.'

The last time I had seen old man Jongilanga looking so discontented was when Skade had told him to sit down. Now I had disappointed the very man who had so much faith in me. Skade's face was beaming with satisfaction as I walked out of the building in shame and embarrassment.

I didn't know where I was going but my legs took me to Dolly's place. She was now staying in a flat for which I paid half the rent. The sight of a silver-grey BMW in the driveway filled me with apprehension. I knocked at the door with the bravado of a police officer in possession of a warrant of arrest. I heard the delicate clink of cups and saucers and I knew Dolly was entertaining a visitor. I couldn't wait for her to open the door and pushed it ajar myself. I was greeted by a cloud of smoke and I knew that whoever the visitor was lacked etiquette. The bravado that had pushed me into the flat fizzled away as I saw that Dolly was entertaining Mr Vabaza, the mayor, my boss in a sense. The two empty cups and the ashtray filled with cigar *stompies* on the coffee table told me that they had been there for a while. They were sitting on a couch with Dolly's back to the door. I was considering turning and walking away when Mr Vabaza jokingly said.

'Hey, Mr Limba, why do you keep following me everywhere? Or have I forgotten we had an appointment?' I was startled to learn that the old man felt my presence in the house because I had tried to walk as quietly as possible.

'Mr Mayor, the door was open so I just came in,' I said apologetically. 'I'm here to see Dolly.'

'You want to see me?' Dolly looked at me as if I were a strange creature that had dropped in from another planet. I nodded. I wanted to say 'yes' but appeared to have lost my voice with nervousness.

'Okay, just wait in the kitchen,' Dolly said without looking at me.

I sat in the kitchen wondering what was so urgent that it could not wait until the next working day to discuss in the office. I was growing impatient with waiting but I had to treat the situation with a bit of adult maturity. I had done it before, forced myself to smile even though I carried large bags of depression in my heart.

'Hah, hah, hah, hah . . .'

The thunderous roar of laughter came from the mayor. That laugh of his always irritated me. Whenever he laughed he opened his mouth wide like a braying donkey.

'Huhh, Bongani, heh, heh, heh . . .'

I grew more apprehensive as I heard Dolly addressing the mayor by his first name. As I sat there I felt a lump of bitterness growing inside me. I began to wonder if Dolly had been surreptitiously performing unsavoury acts with the mayor. I tiptoed towards the lounge and as I peeped through the door I saw the old man holding Dolly's hand in the way that a loving husband would do. The sight spurred me into action and my gentlemanly propensities flew out the window. The next thing I remember is that I was in the lounge.

'Dolly, I cannot wait any longer. Please can I see you in the kitchen right now?'

'Can I?' she said to the old man, gently pulling him by his long goatee.

'Well, seeing that the young man is in such a hurry, why not?'

I unleashed my fury as we entered the kitchen.

'Dolly, what are you doing with this old man?'

'What do you mean what am I doing? Don't you know what lovers do?'

'C'mon Dolly, you can't call that man your lover. He is old enough to be your father!' I had raised my voice.

'I can't believe you just said that. Have you forgotten that you have a wife to go home to? Themba, please leave and stop bothering me in my house.' The tone of her voice revealed annoyance.

'Dolly, you can't treat me like this. I pay half of the rent here.'

'Well, who do you think pays the other half, eh?'

'Oh, now I see. This is all about money. You are doing this because the old man has promised you a promotion.'

'Themba, I do not have time for this. Just leave!' she said, and walked back to the lounge.

I was convinced that Dolly did not have feelings for the man but somehow material concerns thrived over human dignity. She had allowed him to visit her, to touch her and probably sleep with her for the sake of securing a job. I followed Dolly and found the old man still sitting cozily on the couch. He looked like an old fat chimpanzee. My palms were sweating as I stood in front of him trying to suppress the urge to tear his protruding belly open with the knife that was on the table. The fat that filled his stomach was surely enough to feed the whole of Sekunjalo.

'You . . .' I said, pointing at him. I bit my lower lip trying to control the words coming out of my mouth.

'You will cry some day!' My voice was a bit shaky, betraying the anger that had filled me up to the throat.

'Young man, please don't be disrespectful to me. I will not tolerate your childish remarks,' he said in a low relaxed voice as if nothing had happened.

It was clear that I had lost Dolly to him but I was determined not to lose my temper. Loss of temper leads to abnormal behaviour. A man who behaves abnormally has no dignity. A man with no dignity is not a man.

There was no use in me trying to compete with the mayor with regard to power and material resources. He had the power to frustrate me by suppressing my ideas and the views I expressed on behalf of my community. But that did not mean I was going to withdraw or change the ideals that I stood for. I may have been the poorer man in terms of material resources, but I was rich with pride and integrity. Anything I could buy for Dolly he could buy twice over, but my humility was not for sale.

Bongani Vabaza appeared to be the winner because he had the authority and the money, but that did not make me a loser. I believe in the premise that to compromise under certain circumstances does not make me a weak man. Compromise is not always a bad thing. It is at times the best thing. It is better to compromise a situation than to compromise an idea, for a man and his idea are inseparable. To challenge an idea is to challenge the man. I shall not compromise my ideas.

When I walked away from Dolly's flat, I knew I was never going to retrace my steps. My experience that day had taught me that she lacked self respect, and I did not want to associate with such a woman.

10

A man of power

I believe in my people's saying that the greatness of a man is not measured by the size of his body or the number of days he has lived, but by his achievements in his lifetime. In a very short space of time I had risen to become a respectable figure in the community. I had become the headmaster. The principal. The highest ranked official in a school. The recent developments in my life surely secured me a place among the great men in our society.

Occupying Miss Phatheka's seat remained beyond my wildest dreams until the moment I set foot inside the office on the first school day of the year. That Monday is a day that will never escape my mind. I remember it very clearly. I spent the whole morning admiring my new office. The furniture was new and spotless; the fan blew cool air; the chair was so comfortable I felt like sleeping in it. I sat by the window watching children as they played in the schoolyard. I went back to my chair, sat cross-legged and whistled a tune. I swung the chair until I felt somewhat nauseous. Stop! I swung it once more. Stop it! Why was I doing it again?

I had to start working. What do principals do in the office? I was not sure but I had to do something. There was a new post being advertised. I had to go through the applications – that's the work I could do. While browsing through the letters and CVs I came across a name that seemed familiar: Thandi Maduna. Where had I heard that name before?

I read her CV and discovered that she had also been to Fort Hare between 1991 and 1995. Now I remembered her! Thandi was a girl I had admired greatly. I had come very close to finding myself immersed between her legs. The only obstacle was that she had discovered that I had a baby with Thuli who was in the hinterlands of the old Transkei homeland at the time. It was so unfair that I had to lose a girl I loved as a result of an act of careless conception. Thuli had just begun her studies in social work at the University of Transkei. All I wanted was companionship while studying at the University of Fort Hare. I moved heaven and earth trying to convince Thandi but she wouldn't comply. My promises to dump Thuli made things even worse. Thandi began giving me one of those feminist lectures that always irritate me.

'How foolish do you think I am? Do you expect me to take pleasure in destroying another woman?' she said with her hands on her hips.

'Thandi, you are not destroying any relationship. This woman you are talking about deliberately fell pregnant to remain with me,' I said, trying to convince her.

'Oh, I see. She climbed on top of herself and got pregnant,' Thandi said in the most sarcastic manner.

'Thandi, please don't take it that way.' I tried to calm her down.

'Themba, it's simple: you have a relationship and I don't wish to be a party in destroying it. If you want to leave your woman don't use me as an excuse to do so.'

She reminded me of Miss Thekiso, my old schoolteacher who always argued, 'A woman who willingly destroys another woman's house is destroying herself in the process'.

I am usually a very persistent man when it comes to persuading a woman, but Thandi's arrogance left me no room to discuss the issue further. She ended up falling into the hands of Bheki, a rural boy from KwaNongoma, in the hinterlands of KwaZulu-Natal.

The same woman was now looking for a job in my school. It's true that a foot never sniffs its path. The same woman who had vehemently refused me was now writing letters begging for a job in my school. Now it was my turn

to play hide and seek, but eventually she would be wrapped around my finger – that's one of the fringe benefits of being in authority. I picked up the phone and dialled her number. It rang a couple of times and then a voice on the other side answered, 'Thandi, hello.'

'Hello, Thandi, how are you?' I said, conscious of keeping my voice as calm as possible.

'I'm fine, thanks. Who's speaking?' She was breathing heavily against the phone.

'It's Mr Limba. Mr Themba Limba, the principal of Sinethemba High School.'

'Mr Themba who?' she said inquisitively.

'Themba Limba, the principal of Sinethemba High School,' I said, putting emphasis on the word 'principal' so that she could understand the powers bestowed upon me.

'Are you the same Themba Limba I know from Fort Hare?'

'The one and only,' I said proudly.

'Themba, it's you! Oh, how are you? You are a principal now. Some people have made progress, you know.' She began speaking incoherently, like an underdog athlete who had unexpectedly won a race.

'Yeah, I'm calling in connection with your job application.'

'Oh, do I stand any chance of being employed?'

'I'm afraid there's a pile of applications here in front of me. You'll be lucky if you get shortlisted for an interview. Besides, we are looking for an experienced teacher. As far as I can determine from your CV, you haven't been employed since you left school. I see that you did get a temporary post for three months while another teacher was on maternity leave. And that you've been doing voluntary work. That's it! It's not enough to convince me that you can handle a classroom full of children.'

'Oh please, Themba . . .'

As she spoke I could feel my heart floating in ecstasy. I began to swing from side to side in my chair. The same mouth that had said, 'I can't love you', was now saying 'please' to me. I find it most enjoyable to hear a beautiful woman begging me for something. It is always fun to put on an act even though I give in eventually.

'I am so desperate to get that post. My mother is a pensioner and my two brothers are still at school. I really need a job.'

'Well, we'll see what happens. So far you haven't convinced me that you really want this post. Perhaps we'll have to meet and talk about it. You'll hear from me now that I've got your number.'

'All right, I'll hear from you, then. Bye.'

I could only imagine that she spent a few minutes contemplating her dilemma. She was desperate to get the job but a lack of adequate working experience was her major obstacle, and yet she needed a job in order to gain experience.

I had never tried to convince a girl about my feelings as much as I had with Thandi. She had repeatedly refused me even though I knew that deep down she had strong feelings for me. She could not resist the electric current that sparked between us as our lips touched on that fateful night after the sports awards dinner at Fort Hare. We were voted as the best-dressed couple of the evening. As part of our celebration we went to my room in Beda House, where we sat and talked until the early hours. It was in my room that she found herself submitting to my warm embrace. It was also there that she confessed her true feelings for me.

'I do love you, Themba. But I can't allow my feelings to dominate my thinking. I know we don't have a future together,' she argued.

'What do you mean we don't have a future together? You know that I love you Thandi. I'd do anything to be with you,' I said in a low voice. It was one of those romantic moments when couples whisper to one another and speak closely to each other's ears.

'Themba, you are in a relationship and, above all, you are a father.'

'Thandi, you've just admitted that you love me. Why don't you just follow your heart and be with me?'

'I will not allow myself to be driven by emotions. A woman whose emotions dominate her reasoning is quick to lose her virtue.'

I had heard that lecture from old man Jongilanga before. He had been speaking at the funeral of an old woman. Part of his message to the young women there was, 'A woman without virtue is like a chicken without a head. She blunders all over and falls into the hands of wrong men.'

Clearly Thandi subscribed to this philosophy but now that principle was about to cost her a job.

Hearing Thandi's voice transported me back to my Fort Hare days when I first met her. I was off to my Agriculture lecture when I suddenly saw a curvaceous body in front of me.

I can't help it. I find it divinely pleasurable to view the structure of a woman's body from the rear. Whenever a beautiful woman passes, I can't help the temptation to turn and look at what she has to offer from the back. My wife has smacked me several times in public because of this. At one stage she even threatened to smash my testicles.

Thandi was appropriately endowed with flesh on the most interesting regions of her body. The sway of her body and the jiggle of her hips underneath tight jeans made my blood run amok. I made a vow to myself that someday I would have my fingerprints all over her body. I always get what I want or else I do not have the blood of the AmaMpandla clan running in my veins.

Thandi refused me several times but I was not a man to give up easily. A man who is outwitted by a woman not only dishonours himself, but also denigrates the dignity of manhood. For a man's strength is measured by his ability to melt even a heart of stone. In my endeavours to find a way into Thandi's heart, I had resorted to the level of simple friendship to maintain our relationship. I knew from experience that friendship could work wonders.

On the night of the sports awards dinner Bheki was away and Thandi agreed to go with me as a friend. I had planned the move very well, just like a hyena moving in on the prey when the lion is away. I invited Thandi to my room and showed her all my sports awards as well as my photo album. Of course, I had already taken out all the photos that contained Thuli. I sat next to her explaining the photos and my sporting achievements. I gradually moved closer to her and casually put my left arm across her shoulders. I could feel the warmth on my left-hand side as my thigh rubbed against hers. I gently caressed her back, moved slowly underneath her left armpit and tenderly squeezed her nipple. Seeing that there was no objection, I closed the photo album and drew her closer to my body. Her supple breasts pressed against my chest. I touched her soft lips with mine. Her lips were slightly parted and her breath was warm. Luther Vandross provided the musical background. The song 'Power of Love' set the appropriate mood for the scene. I was convinced that the song had done the trick when Thandi exclaimed, 'Oh, this song!'

'What, babe, do you like it?' I asked boastfully, feeling somewhat proud of myself.

'Yes,' she said, and looked me straight in the eyes. 'It reminds me of Bheki!'

I felt a lump of bitterness and regret growing inside me. The girl could not speak without that Zulu boy's shadow looming over her head. My overtures had once again been unsuccessful.

Now that same girl was almost ready to lick my feet – just to get a job.

The district office sent a representative to oversee the selection process as we shortlisted candidates for interviews. Miss Rhasana was a tall and large woman with grey hair showing under the wig she always wore. She was famous for her strong feminist principles and her heavy hand against men.

No wonder she had not gone down the aisle yet. Her pair of thick glasses rested on her large flat nose. The presence of this woman in my school undermined both my power as the principal and, above all, my integrity as a man.

There were over 300 applicants, 200 of whom were presently unemployed. The selection panel decided to choose six applicants for interviews. In closing the session, old man Jongilanga said, 'We have now reached the end of our selection process. All the candidates that we have selected are unemployed and have in many ways demonstrated their commitment in uplifting their communities. Now, the next level is the crucial one where the candidates have to come personally and tell us what they can do for the community of Sinethemba. Son of Gwebani, I must leave it in your capable hands to ensure that these candidates will be here on the day of the interview. There I stop.'

'I'll be pleased to call the candidates, old man, thank you,' I said, trying very hard to sound polite.

I was keen to call them because among the shortlisted individuals was Thandi. I picked up the phone immediately after the selection panel had left my office.

'Thandi, hello,' she answered the phone with lots of enthusiasm.

'Hey, Thandi, it's me, Themba. How are you today?' My voice was lively, revealing that I was the bearer of good news.

'Hi, I'm okay, Themba, and you?'

'I'm well.' I paused briefly, giving her a chance to lead the conversation.

'Please tell me you have selected me for an interview.'

'Well, it's been difficult because I'm not alone on the selection panel. But I tried to convince them that you used to be a hard worker at Fort Hare,' I said, trying to keep her in suspense.

'And, what did they say, Themba?' she asked with undisguised anxiety.

'*Ja*, they had to agree because your good results also supported my opinion.'

'Oh, that's wonderful news. You know, it is so hard even to get an interview these days. When you are desperate for a job you even get satisfaction from receiving a rejection letter rather than having to wait without a clue as to what is happening.'

'You have to be here on Wednesday morning at ten thirty for the interview,' I said, trying to stick to the purpose of the call.

'I'll definitely be there, Themba. Thank you.'

'See you then, bye.'

As I put the phone down, I looked at the list and discovered that I did not recognise any of the other names. Besides, all of the other candidates were men. I called all of them but was not interested in listening to their anxieties and curious questions.

On the day of the interview the sight of Thandi brought back memories of my university days. She looked as good as, if not better than, the last time I had seen her. I had to show her what a powerful person I had become. Power is one of the major attributes used to measure a man's integrity. A man who cannot exercise power cannot be trusted to protect his family and his dignity as a man. I sent the school governing body members this way and that, hoping that Thandi would notice how powerful I had become.

'Bring my file; take all my calls because I'm in a meeting; hurry up because I have another meeting.'

Looking back at my performance, Thandi probably noticed my actions and said to herself that some things never change. While we were at university I used to visit her after soccer training and fill her room with the suffocating stench of human sweat and dirty football socks. It was all done with the intention of reminding her that I was a good soccer player. Those overtures were not successful then, but now she needed a job.

For some reason I did not have too many questions for Thandi during the interview. As I sat there I felt deep-seated emotions for her. Every time I looked at her face my mind wandered back to the days when we were still students. My reminiscences were disturbed by the ever-present memory of

Bheki, the Zulu dog that had laid his paws on her. I still could not forgive her for that.

After the interviews the panel decided on Thandi as the right candidate for the job. In motivating the panel's decision, old man Jongilanga argued, 'This girl from the AmaHlubi people is a learned woman. She attended school at the university that many leaders of Africa went to – the University of Fort Hare. The daughter of Maduna has demonstrated her commitment by doing voluntary work. To her, teaching is not just a job but also a profession that she has come to live. She is dedicated in serving her society.'

It was amazing that old man Jongilanga knew so much and held so many leadership positions in the community in spite of being as illiterate as my father who had not even known how to hold a pen.

I called Thandi immediately after the meeting adjourned.

'Thandi, hello!'

'Hey, Thandi, it's Themba. How are you doing?'

'I'm fine. Tell me you have good news for me.'

'Well, maybe I do, but first you should know that I had to fight for them to employ you. I promised the panel that you wouldn't disappoint.'

'Are you seriously saying that I got the job?' she burst out. Even before she heard my response she continued, 'Oh, that's wonderful! It's the best news I have heard in a long time.'

'You are expected to start working on the first Tuesday after the Easter weekend.'

'Thank you very much, Themba. I will return the favour some day.'

That was not news to me because she wouldn't dare to turn me down again, especially now that I was her boss. Refusing the overtures of your boss is a risky business, especially in a country where there is such a high rate of unemployment.

11

Should a man cry?

I decided not to give immediate chase after Thandi; that would have raised many people's eyebrows. I wanted to give her time to settle and when she began to feel comfortable then I would remind her of my part in taking her out of the sea of poverty. The only salvation for her was to come back to these arms that had once held her so tenderly. Besides, there was never a shortage of opportunities in a school environment.

I had been entertaining schoolgirls who boast more delicate flesh than that of their worn-out teachers. I had never taken a particular interest in schoolchildren, but what is a man supposed to do when girls with tender and fresh bodies present their womanhood to him? Is he supposed to say, no, I can't touch your body because I prefer that of your older sister who has probably had several lives coming out of her womb? How is it possible that a man can refuse the solid bodies and opt for the large loose-limbed ones in whose veins blood often competes with alcohol.

As a schoolboy I had been one of the staunch campaigners against the association of teachers with their female students. Young and sometimes not-so-young teachers obviously had many great advantages over us schoolboys in dealing with girls. We did not have the material resources they did. Schoolgirls were tempted by presents such as money and expensive clothing that male teachers dished out as a way of expressing their interest. Little did my fellow schoolmates and I know the pleasure our educators derived from the young girls' bodies.

As a teacher I have now had the privilege of experiencing the adult's perspective. As I grew up it was impressed upon me that I dare not submit to temptation, but I have always wondered if the same rule applies when temptation is good for you. As an adult I reasoned that the danger is actually in the way in which you submit to temptation. I believe in letting young girls initiate the move; that way they will not reveal it to anyone. This is what happened with a girl called Nosipho. She was in my Grade Ten English class. The creator must have worked on a Sunday to carve such a beauty. She had big brown eyes and her dark brown skin was smooth. Her face was plump, with dimples in both cheeks. She was appropriately moulded with slender legs, round thighs and extra flesh on her hips. She had a flat stomach and small firm breasts.

Having been married for a long time I could not suppress my appetite for young and fresh thighs. My sexual desire for young girls had been spawned by Thuli's inability to look after her weight. Her large bosom and the rings of flesh on her body, especially the folds on her stomach, killed my sexual appetite for her. My hormones had become more attuned to the soft and tender bodies of young girls.

In our schools in the townships, a single teacher is usually responsible for all sporting codes, including recreational activities. Because of my own activism in sports during my school and university days, I had to be responsible for sports in our school. I must hasten to declare that I was quite loath to take on this responsibility because I found my mind being clouded by the fringe benefits that were to come my way as a result.

Soon other male teachers began to envy my privileged status as the sports teacher due to the pleasures I derived from watching netball. It was beyond any man's imagination. You see, the best legs in a school are usually seen at the netball games. Netball players usually have solid, long and well cared for legs, which only a sexually impotent man would not find arousing. The astounding spectacle of young girls in short netball skirts that from time to time flew up to expose a full view of their panties made the sport more exciting and I gave it preference over rugby and soccer most of the time. The young girls would jump very high, spreading their legs wide apart even if there was no need to do so. The netball kit and the short skirts that the girls wore as the school uniform often provoked my hormones and I got vigorous reaction from down below.

Nosipho was wearing one of those short uniform skirts when she approached me one afternoon.

'I'm sorry, sir, do you have a minute? I would like to talk to you in private?'

I could tell by the look in her eyes that she had something very intimate to share.

'In private? Well, it depends on what you want to talk about.'

'No, I just . . . you see . . . I would like to talk to you about something . . .'

I noticed the nervousness in the young girl's eyes. My goal was not to embarrass her but to make it clear that I was not the one who had initiated the move.

'Okay, listen . . .' I tried to make things easier for her. 'I won't be able to talk to you now. Why don't you come to my house after school? Here, please buy me a *smiley* and bring it to my house,' I said, giving her a twenty rand note. A *smiley* is half a sheep's head, which was my favourite meal during the day because I was hopeless in the cooking department. I knew it was safer to see her during the day because Thuli always came back late from work. She preferred to visit her clients, mostly abused women and children, in the evenings in order to meet the whole family.

Nosipho arrived with the *smiley* and I called her into the bedroom so we could 'talk in private'. I closed the bedroom door behind her and began to touch her tender body.

'Teacher, no . . . I wanted . . . Teacher, please stop . . .'

'C'mon, I'll be gentle. I'm not like the schoolboys.' I had to make her feel good about what we were about to do. After all, her looks placed her above the league of the schoolboys. A girl with a mature body like hers deserved nothing but the best, and the best was me.

'Please wait, teacher. I wanted to . . . oh . . .'

I closed her girlish pleas with a kiss. I had been in the game for long enough to know that 'no' could sometimes mean the opposite. I had met girls who'd always pretend not to have an interest in me when it was actually their wildest dream to have me on top of them. A touch here and there and Nosipho's objections had disappeared. Her body had become less rigid and I knew I had reduced her into longing and craving for me. As I cut through her supple thighs I could tell that another man had been travelling the same path quite regularly. She was now moaning with ecstasy in between telling me to stop. At the end of it I lay next to her feeling satisfied, rejuvenated, a man reborn.

At that moment of near oblivion I heard what sounded like my wife's car. I looked out through the window and saw it was already in the driveway. Thuli had come home early from work. I jumped up and put on my clothes. I thrust a fifty rand note into Nosipho's hand and motioned her to get out through the kitchen door.

Whenever I looked at Nosipho after this encounter an electric shock ran through my body, eliciting a vigorous reaction in my pants. She also found it difficult to look me in the eyes. The few minutes she had spent on my bed were obviously so pleasurable that they could not escape her mind.

That was a year ago and so much has changed since then. My longing for Nosipho has since been obliterated by her mounting readiness to open her thighs for any man. She was definitely above consorting with schoolboys.

There was a taxi driver who regularly picked her up after school. His VW Microbus was known in the township for playing all the recent hits. He played them so loudly that everyone knew from a distance that he was approaching. Most young people liked his taxi because of his fast driving and the music he played. He would hoot and wave to every girl he passed on the way. The passenger seat was reserved exclusively for girls. He would press and pinch their thighs as he changed gears.

Soon other cars driven by different men could be seen visiting Nosipho. She was often seen at The Ladies' Joint, a very popular shebeen among young people. In that shebeen even the wimpiest man found a woman to warm his bed. Men who drank there were gentlemen too. They never fought over a woman. True socialists. They lived according to the principle, 'What is yours is not yours; it's ours'. So they exchanged women and some men even shared the same woman in one night. If you had one today, don't bother to look for her tomorrow. It was no big deal to get another; just fill the table with beer. MaDlamini, the owner of the shebeen, had built some rooms in the back yard. She let people rent a room for an hour or two, or even for the whole night. The rates for the rooms varied depending on how many customers wished to occupy the same room at the same time, and according to the time of the month. The prices often increased at the end of the month because most people had money then. Nosipho was apparently one of the major attractions in this shebeen. Even the owner held her in high regard because she usually brought in a mass of male customers.

It is not usually easy for me to let go of a woman once I have experienced the throes of passion with her. But I had to force Nosipho out of my system. Association with this former beauty of the township became something of an embarrassment. That is the risk involved when you have dealings with this age group that still harbours ambitions of exploring with their bodies.

Sometimes it is wiser to stick to more mature women even though they can be a nuisance with their unending ambitions and demands. They always confuse sexual entertainment with a relationship. Where a relationship does exist, they assume it will translate into marriage, forgetting that life is more complex than this.

There is a saying among my people that a bird can fly high but it has to come to the ground for food. This seemed to be justified when Thandi came to my office looking deeply distressed. This was the moment I had been waiting for for all these years.

'Hey, Miss Maduna, what can I do for you this morning? You know, I've been meaning to talk to you,' I said, in order to break the ice for her.

'I wish to discuss a matter outside the school curriculum with you,' she said in a low voice. I knew immediately that it was a very intimate subject that she needed us to talk about.

'I also wanted to chat to you along those lines,' I said, and got up to close the door. She was still facing the direction of my chair. She stood there like a little girl who is too shy to say 'yes' to a boy. I stood behind her and began to caress her shoulders gently. I came closer, ready to start kissing her neck. I could smell her sweet perfume. It was the same one she used to wear as a student.

'You know, since you came to this school I've been thinking about our days at Fort Hare. We had really good times together. No woman has ever made me happy in the way that you did. I may be married now, but my heart still longs for you, Thandi.' I was brave enough to say these words because she was not looking at me. She was a woman with very penetrating eyes. Whenever she looked at me she looked through me. I felt like she could see what was inside me, which was usually different from what came out of my mouth.

'Well, that is not what I was hoping to discuss with you,' she said, pushing my hands off her shoulders and turning to look at me. 'Do you know Nosipho from the Grade Eleven class?'

'Nosipho, you mean . . .' Suddenly something choked my throat and no words could come out. What came to my mind was that Thandi might have discovered that my manhood had once fumbled between Nosipho's thighs.

'Oh yeah, I know her. I taught her. What is she saying?' I asked absentmindedly.

'She came to me to discuss her problem.'

'What problem is she having now? She has to spend more time on her books if she wants to pass,' I said, trying to keep away from the subject of our rendezvous in my bedroom.

'No, it's not schoolwork. Her problem is social and it affects her performance at school.' She was coming to what I feared most.

'Thandi, since when did you become a social worker? We employed you here to be a Business Economics teacher; you should have nothing to do with learners' social problems.' I had always found it easy to play a reverse psychology trick on the female species, but clearly Thandi was not a woman to be easily outwitted or diverted.

'Mr Limba, this child is a victim of abuse.'

'So, are you trying to accuse me of . . .?' I stammered with nervousness.

'I'm not accusing anybody. All I'm saying is that this child shared her problem with me because she did not know who else to turn to. The perpetrator is her uncle.'

'Oh, is that so?' I felt relieved because I had thought that the perpetrator was me. I was devastated because that would have jeopardised my chances with Thandi. Even worse, my reputation as a school principal and community leader was at stake. Thandi narrated the story of abuse to which I listened as attentively as a concerned parent.

Apparently both Nosipho's parents were serving long-term sentences in prison for offences that did not interest me at the time. Nosipho had been staying at her grandmother's place. With the support of her son, Banzi, Nosipho's grandmother did her best to make sure that her granddaughter got everything she wanted. Nosipho had always shared her problems with her grandmother until the problem concerned her grandmother's son.

Nosipho told Thandi that Banzi had come home drunk one Friday night. He had passed out on the floor next to Nosipho who slept on a homemade grass mat in the room that was used as a kitchen during the day. In the middle of the night Banzi had rolled towards Nosipho and started fondling her thighs.

'What are you doing, uncle?' Nosipho exclaimed.

'Sh-sh-sh! You gonna wake them,' Banzi had said.

'Uncle stop!'

'Shut up!' Banzi said, and closed Nosipho's mouth with his massive hand that almost suffocated her with the stench of tobacco. With the other hand he reached for her southern hemispheres and held her so tightly that she could barely move her head. The suffocation was soon followed by a sharp pain between her legs. The pain lasted for what seemed like eternity as the man breathed heavily on top of her. Her sobs did not persuade Uncle Banzi to stop. Nosipho wanted to scream but she did not know what people's reaction would be. Besides, this was the very uncle who bought the food that she ate every day. As she lay there feeling the pain, Nosipho heard his drunken footsteps as Banzi stumbled across the room in the darkness. He walked to his bedroom where Joyce, his wife, lay in a deep sleep. From that night on, Uncle Banzi's visits to Nosipho's bed were almost constant whenever his wife was not around.

Nosipho thought about sharing her predicament with Aunt Joyce but decided against it because that could cost her a home. Joyce would not destroy her marriage because of a loose-thighed girl. All of Nosipho's friends had been kicked in their chests by horses, making it impossible for them to keep a secret, so she could not confide in them over such a sensitive matter.

Uncle Banzi's visits had continued for over two years until finally Nosipho had decided to tell Thandi about what was happening. As Thandi spoke, it crossed my mind that this might have been the private business that Nosipho had wanted us to talk about on the day of our rendezvous. But my genitals had prevailed as the dominant force in my thinking.

'So, what do you think we should do about this now?' I asked. I wasn't sure if it was a good idea to press legal charges against the uncle because somewhere down the line I could be implicated as part of the same act.

'The story doesn't end there. Nosipho is now HIV-positive.'

'What? How? I mean, are you sure?' I could not hide my shock.

'She took the test and brought me the results yesterday.'

'Well, she must go then. We cannot allow someone like that to be in this school.'

'Why not? She is as human as everybody else in this place. After all, you don't know how many people live with the disease here.'

'It doesn't matter! She must go and if anybody else has AIDS, they must also leave this school,' I said firmly.

'You know what, if she goes I am going too. She is HIV-positive and so am I,' Thandi said, looking me straight in the eyes.

'Miss Maduna, this is no joke. If you don't know how to amuse a man you had better twist your knees. I have work to do.'

I took a red pen and pretended to read the script in front of me. Thandi stood there, staring at me, while I kept my eyes fixed on the paper. No one spoke but I could hear her heavy breathing, which revealed her fury. If only she had understood what the news meant to me. Then I heard her turning and walking towards the door. Each footstep was like a hummer punching a nail into my heart. I tried to focus on the paper in front of me but I could not read a thing. The presence of Thandi's perfume in my office inflicted more pain on me. All I could see was Nosipho, begging me to stop. I bowed my head and my pen dropped onto the paper.

12

A man alone

It was ironic that Thandi, the woman who not so long ago was willing to lick my feet to get a job, had become a real thorn in my professional life. She had the audacity to lodge a case at the Department of Education district office claiming that I was sexually harassing her, and that I intended excluding Nosipho from the school because of her HIV status.

Miss Rhasana, who was always hostile to men, jumped at the opportunity. She called an urgent meeting of the school governing body. I knew what they were trying to do – oust me from the school. There was nothing I could do to prevent this from happening. They could take my job away, but I would not allow them to take my pride as well. To save myself from all the embarrassment I decided not to go to the meeting. I did not need to be humiliated by an old man surrounded by a bunch of contemptuous women whose sole desire was to ridicule every bearded creature.

When I arrived at school the following Monday Miss Rhasana was already waiting for me. Her large bosom and amorphous body made her look like a bullfrog as she sat in a chair, and she wore her usual disgustingly red lipstick that was always overapplied.

'Mr Limba, I invited you to a meeting last Friday,' she said, looking over the thick-rimmed glasses that rested on her large, flat nose.

'I know,' I said as I went past her.

'And you did not attend.' She stood up and put her hands on her hips.

'Of course I didn't,' I said, putting my files on the table.

'May I know why not?'

'Because I was not well,' I said, and looked her straight in the eyes.

'May I have a doctor's certificate for that?'

This woman was too sure of herself. I wanted to get rid of that element in her.

'I don't have one,' I said unapologetically.

'Why? Why don't you have a medical certificate if you were not well to the extent of missing such an important meeting?' She had raised her voice.

'Don't yell at me!' I said, and found myself pointing a finger at her face. I was getting a bit emotional, which was not part of the plan. I wanted to frustrate her by showing her that I did not care much about whatever she was to say.

'Well, will you tell me why you do not have a doctor's certificate?' she asked in a very low, strictly controlled but not calm voice.

'Because the traditional doctor does not issue certificates.'

'Mr Limba, I don't have time for silly jokes,' she said sternly, like a schoolteacher reprimanding a naughty boy.

'I don't either. Why don't you stop fooling around and tell me what you came here for?' I was getting agitated and was prepared to hear the worst. My job was at stake and there was nothing I could do to rescue the situation.

'You know, if it were for me to decide, I would be firing you this very moment,' she said, hitting her fist on the table to emphasise her point.

'So, that means I still have my job?' I was amazed.

'From now on you are no longer the acting principal. You are just an ordinary teacher. Miss Maduna is now the acting principal of the school.'

'And why did you choose her? Is it because she hates my guts as much as you do?'

'You know very well that Miss Maduna has shown great commitment to her work in the past year. The yearly reports that you signed as the principal are clear evidence of that,' she explained.

'So it took you a year's report to assess and promote her and only a day's rumour to demote me,' I said, trying to pursue the argument further.

'Mr Limba, I'm the one who called this meeting!' she said emphatically.

'Oh, so this is actually a meeting?' I tried to be sarcastic so that she did not see how frustrated I actually felt.

'I must go,' she said, as she took her file from the table and walked towards the door. 'By the way . . .' She stopped and looked at me as if remembering something that excited her. Then she took out a sealed envelope from her file and handed it over to me. 'This is your first formal warning from the district office. You had better stay away from schoolchildren if it is your intention to keep this job,' she said, and left the office.

'Go to hell!' I felt like saying, but decided against it. At least I still had my job, which was something that I had not expected.

My belief that township gossip is the fastest medium to spread information was reaffirmed that day. It took just a few minutes before it was known all over Sekunjalo that I had been dismissed as the acting principal; people knew even before the announcement was officially made at school. I knew that with strong enemies such as Skade and the mayor my future with the city council was hanging in the balance. So I wrote a resignation letter from my post as a councillor, citing my responsibilities as an educator and a father as too demanding to allow me time for community responsibilities.

Those in the know say the higher you go the harder you fall. A timely jump from the political ladder is the only salvation from a hard fall. But even when you have safely landed, there are vampires that always thirst for your blood.

I thought I was free from troubles until one Thursday afternoon when I came back from work and found Thuli sobbing in the bedroom.

'What's wrong, Thuli?' I asked with astonishment.

'Themba, how could you? How could you, Themba?' she said as she continued wailing.

'How could I what?' I asked with bewilderment. I had committed so many offences in the past and had no idea which one she might be referring to.

'Nosipho. That little girl. How could you do it, Themba? Why? Don't I satisfy you?'

'Oh, that, I mean, you see, ehmm . . . That girl must be crazy. Who said I did anything to her?' I was caught off-guard and did not know how to react.

'She told me everything.' She retorted.

'What, what everything? She's lying. I didn't do anything to her. What did she tell you?' I tried to deny matters even though it was clear that Thuli had received information from a reliable source.

'She came to me,' Thuli said, wiping her tears with the back of her hand. 'She came to me for counselling. She's my client.'

Damn, there was no evading that one. A client has to reveal everything to a counsellor for therapy purposes. I knew that Nosipho would not have left out any detail regarding our encounter.

'Thuli, listen. Okay, I was tempted because she seduced me, but nothing happened.'

'Knowing you, do you think I'm gonna believe that?'

'Thuli, please believe me. Nothing happened.'

'Whether you slept with her or not is not the issue now. The concern is, given the fact that you get tempted when "seduced", we need to be sure that there are no health risks involved between the two of us.'

'What do you mean, Thuli?' I asked with agitation.

'Let's go for an HIV test,' she said emphatically.

'What? I mean, do you think it's really necessary?' I did not know what to say.

'It's either that or I leave with my children.'

'C'mon, Thuli. Listen . . . I mean, I'm strong and there's nothing wrong with me.'

'I don't know about that. Only the doctors can tell,' she said relentlessly.

'Thuli, you know I love you . . .' I tried to play with her emotions. When all else fails, the trick is to tell your woman all the things she loves to hear.

'You probably said those words on the day you forced yourself on that little girl!'

'Do you really think that I forced myself on her? Thuli, you know very well that I am not a rapist. Aren't you supposed to be on my side here?' I tried to twist things around in her mind.

'Perhaps I'd be on your side if you had told me the truth before I could find out.'

'So you don't want to believe me?' I said with a twinge of sadness in my voice.

'Let's go for a test,' she said sternly.

'Thuli, please . . .'

'Just know that I'll only return to this house when we both get tested for HIV.' She said it with finality, as if stating a commandment of modern marriage.

'Well, suit yourself!' I said for lack of anything else to say and went straight to the bedroom. A few minutes later she joined me in bed.

It was one of those nights when a married couple seems like two strangers sharing the same bed. There was an invisible border in the middle of the bed as we both avoided getting close to one another. I knew I had married a woman of her word who could be very stubborn at times, but I was hoping she would forget her promise.

The next morning I left for work as usual. When I got home in the afternoon it was to an empty house. Thuli had collected up and taken everything that she had ever bought. Our framed wedding photo next to the bed was the only reminder that I had once been a happy man, a family man. I looked at it as

I lay on my back. I thought about the day I had first expressed my feelings to her on a hot Wednesday afternoon. I still remembered it as if it were yesterday. Zakes had made it his business to see to it that I was introduced to under-waist pleasures. Thuli's beauty was very inviting even though I was a bit wary to indulge in the forbidden fruits under the guidance of my notorious cousin. Her smile was captivating, her eyes shone and her teeth glowed like a galaxy of stars behind her thin soft lips.

It was during the afternoon study time and Zakes had told Thuli that our English teacher wanted to see her in the classroom. As soon as she entered the room, Zakes locked the door and there we were, Thuli and I, the two of us locked in the same room. Well, luck was not on my side that day, but I persisted until one fateful day a year later. I had been walking her home every day after school and carried her books for her. Even this made me feel good, for other boys wished for the opportunity to walk next to such a beauty. I appreciated the hugs I got each time I was about to leave. The thought of touching Thuli's breasts haunted my dreams to the extent that I would be forced to wake up at night and change my underwear. It took a year before I could turn those dreams into reality. The hugs extended to kisses, and the rest is history.

Now that woman was breaking up with me after so many years of marriage. She had left me because of one stupid move. Where is the justice in this world? How could I lose the woman of my dreams over a single meaningless encounter? It was nothing more than a sexual exploration and did not involve any emotions. But now that single encounter was costing me my family and, at worst, it could cost me my life. And if by any chance I was infected, I would have surely transmitted the virus to my wife who had been so loyal to me for all these years. My heart pounded heavily in my chest. I felt hot liquid rolling down from my eyes and reaching my ears as I lay on my back. I wiped the tears with the back of my hand.

I looked at the photo. Thuli was smiling. I was also smiling. We were happy to be together. Are we both happy to stay apart? I asked myself. I surely was not. What about Thuli? Why was it so easy for her to leave me for such a petty reason? Just because I didn't want to go for an HIV test meant that she would sacrifice our marriage? Could it be possible there was another man in her life? Could Thuli get naked for another man, allow him to touch her body and . . . damn!

I jumped from the bed and our framed photo fell onto the floor and broke into two. I took another look at the photo frame. The light reflected on the broken glass and I saw two versions of myself in the glass. I put it back next to the bed and lay on top of the blankets again. My wife was not here. My children were not here. I did not want to think that another man could be making love to Thuli at that very moment.

The alarm clock went off and it was six in the morning. I did not know when I had fallen asleep. My wife was not here. My children were not here. I did not have anyone to talk to. I switched on the radio and flipped through the channels but none of them interested me. They were either playing irritating music or having lousy discussions about HIV and AIDS, which annoyed me more than ever before. I switched the radio off, sat on the bed and continued with my thoughts. I did not feel like going to school; in fact, I did not feel like leaving the house.

I looked at the clock on the wall and the time was seven fifteen. I had thirty minutes before school started so I took a quick shower. All my shirts were unironed. Even if I had known how to press my clothes, I could not have ironed them just before school started. I put on the same shirt I had worn the previous day and off I went, arriving at school ten minutes late. After the morning prayer Thandi came to me and called me to her office with such arrogant authority that you would have sworn she had been a principal all her life.

'Mr Limba, can I see you in my office right now?' she said, and left without waiting for my response.

'Fine, you'll see me,' I said irritably as I followed her to her office.

As I entered the room Thandi was sitting on the other side of the desk, where I used to sit when I was still at the helm of the school. I sat down in the chair opposite her.

'Mr Limba, do you have any personal problems that you would like to share with me?' Her voice revealed strong emotions behind the question.

'You've just said "personal"; would that still apply if I shared them with you?'

'Mr Limba, I am trying to be of assistance to you here.'

'Well, don't bother!'

'Mr Limba, I am concerned about the decline of your work standard.'

'That's your problem, can I go now?' I did not wait for her response. I just got up and left. As I opened the door she called me again.

'Mr Limba . . .'

'What now?' I could not hide my annoyance.

'Has your wife left you?' she asked.

'How is that any of your business?'

'Because you are my subordinate.'

'Well, you'd better find out from whoever told you.'

'No one told me,' she said after a brief pause. As I turned to go she continued, 'It's the greasy neckline of your shirt that tells everyone.'

I deliberately banged the door as I left the principal's office. She had spoiled my day and I did not have the energy to go to the class where I was meant to have the first period of the day.

'Hey, young girl. Come here,' I said, calling one of the young girls at school.

'Yes sir!' she said, without coming closer to hear what I wanted to say.

'I said come here!' I insisted. She took one step closer but still left a considerable gap between us. I could see in her big eyes she was terrified that I might pounce on her like a lion attacking an antelope. This is the reputation I have built for myself, was the thought that ran through my mind.

'Can you get my files from the Grade Eleven "C" classroom?'

'Yes, sir!' she said, and ran off to the class.

My mere presence in the school premises was increasingly becoming something of an embarrassment. But I did not want to go home either. The loneliness was killing me. I walked out of the schoolyard. I did not know where I was going but I needed to be out of the schoolyard. I was on my own. I had lost everything. I had only my pride to defend.

13

A man apart

I walked blindly out of the schoolyard. As I went past the Apostolic Church I saw old man Jongilanga busy raking the leaves that blanketed the lawn after they had been shaken from the branches by the violent autumn winds. Smoke was pouring from his pipe like a steam train. I found myself turning every second to check that he had not noticed me.

I thought I had managed to evade him when I heard a voice calling me, 'Themba.' I ignored it and walked briskly ahead, pretending not to have heard anything.

'Themba, it's me man, why are you walking so fast?' I turned to look and found that it was Sizwe, my colleague, the drunken master himself. Apparently he had been walking behind me since I left the schoolyard. I took another glance at old man Jongilanga and saw he was consumed in his work.

'Hey, Sizwe, I didn't notice you.' I tried to flash a grin hoping he would not notice how distressed I was.

'I've been walking behind you all the way. Where are you off to?' he asked, certainly with an agenda in mind. It was a badly kept secret that Sizwe had to attend extra classes at The Ladies' Joint at strategic times of the week.

'I'm, eh, I'm going to my wife, you see . . . I have to do some stuff.' I could not make sense of what my mouth was saying.

'Come on, what stuff is that on a Friday afternoon? Come hang out with other men and we can talk about serious issues,' he said as he kept walking towards The Ladies' Joint.

'What serious issues?' I asked, following him and getting curious.

'Man, people talk out there,' he said sternly.

'Talk about what?' So many things had happened that I didn't know which one the gossip heralds would currently consider to be the main news item.

'Man, people talk out there. You'll never know what's going on in the community around you because all you do is lock yourself in that house of yours.' Clearly he was not in a hurry to tell me about what people were saying and I was getting apprehensive.

'What, what are people saying? C'mon tell me, man?'

'Come with me and we'll talk over a glass of beer,' he said.

I followed him into the shebeen, infamous as a symbol of the moral decadence in our society. I had passed the shebeen several times on my way home from school but I never imagined I would set foot on the premises.

We seemed like a pair of lost owls that had blundered into daylight as we walked into the crowded shebeen in suits on a Friday afternoon. Sizwe took his jacket off and rolled the sleeves of his shirt up to the elbows. The owner, MaDlamini, a tall and loose-limbed woman, personally welcomed us and seemed particularly happy to see me.

'All I want is for you boys to enjoy yourselves. You work very hard for the rest of the week and it only makes sense that you reward yourselves and have fun at the end of the week.' I couldn't have agreed more and for a moment I felt like all my sorrows would instantly be history. 'Thanks, thank you, MaDlamini,' we both said.

'So, what can I get you boys?' She was definitely the hospitable type but I knew she would be disappointed when she learned that I did not drink alcohol.

'I'll have the usual, Jack Daniels, and you can get my friend something light, maybe a Savannah Dry,' Sizwe responded.

'No thank you. I don't drink alcohol,' I duly objected.

'C'mon! Where do you come from? Who said Savannah Dry is alcohol?' MaDlamini refuted.

'Themba, please don't embarrass me. Just drink something! Savannah is just a cider,' Sizwe said.

'Okay, okay, not too much of it then. One glass would be fine.' I thought that would be a reasonable compromise.

'Good, now you are talking,' Sizwe said with excitement.

'Let me keep your jackets for you boys.' MaDlamini took our jackets and disappeared into a backroom. The music system was blaring with the kind of contemporary music that I never bothered to listen to. Girls as young as Nozizwe, my first-born, were on the dance floor in a room where you breathed nothing but cigarette smoke. One of the girls kept glancing at me. She was slim and tall with a light complexion and had long and silky artificial hair. She wore a sleeveless blue skimpy blouse that made her stomach public property, flashing a glittering ring in her pierced belly-button. On her left shoulder she had a tattoo that resembled a dolphin, although it had a human face. She had several earrings and even her eyebrows were pierced. By the standard of women in that room she was surely the most attractive, but in my sober state she was not my idea of beauty.

'You see, I knew you would like it here,' Sizwe said. 'You see how that girl is looking at you? Her name is Lungi. She's the hottest thing here.' Sizwe was trying to prompt me to make a move on the girl.

'*Ag* man, I'm not interested in those things any more,' I refuted.

'C'mon man, it's about time you reinvented yourself. Your wife left you, that's it! There's no undoing what you did. All you have to do is move on with your life and become the player that you really are.'

I was beginning to get irritated with Sizwe's comments. 'Sizwe, you can't tell me how to live my life. Yes, my wife and I have very recently separated but you've never been married before.'

At that moment MaDlamini arrived carrying a tray with two bottles and four glasses, the extra two probably meant for possible acquaintances. She put the Jack Daniels in front of Sizwe and the smaller bottle, which contained liquid resembling urine, was placed in front of me. 'There you go boys, enjoy! Just let me know if you need anything else,' MaDlamini offered with a smile. Her large backside jiggled from side to side as she disappeared among the dancing crowd.

'As I was saying,' Sizwe continued, 'I am married to Jack Daniels.' He lifted the bottle high in the air. 'My bottle never disappoints and it will never leave me.' He kissed the bottle before pouring half a glass of the whisky. 'I tell you, my brother. This . . .'

'Man, you had better tell me what you dragged me here for, because I'm not in the mood to discuss my marriage with you!' I said sternly.

'You see, you are doing it again.' He took a huge gulp from the glass, closed his eyes and shook his head vigorously. 'Yes! That's what I'm talking about. It goes exactly to where I send it. This is gonna be a beautiful day.'

'I'm listening, man. You were telling me about what people say.' I was getting impatient with him because I knew that once the whisky had made its impact on his head Sizwe would not make any sense.

'You know what your mistake was? You turned your back on your friends. Remember the saying: "never turn your back on your people".' He released a deep belch. 'That's what you did. It was a big mistake. But fortunately, all is not lost. I'm a good man. I welcome you back. Let's drink to that,' he said, giving another huge belch and holding his glass high. Just at that moment the music system stopped playing. The room went dead quiet and everybody looked in the same direction. Skade and two boys stood next to the music system.

'You irresponsible scumbags, our people are suffering and all you do is sit here and consume the white man's liquor on a Friday afternoon,' an angry Skade shouted. 'Many of you should be at school either as teachers or as learners.'

For a moment everyone was struck dumb and then MaDlamini responded on our behalf.

'Who the hell do you think you are coming into my establishment and disturbing my customers?' She seemed ready to fight for her customers, or should I say the money that her customers were bringing.

'I am here to tell everyone to come to a community meeting at the Apostolic Church now. Old man Jongilanga, the elder of the community, is bereaved. We cannot fold our arms when the community is perishing.' Skade spoke in a high voice, putting emphasis on his words as if he were addressing a crowd at a rally. With that he beckoned his companions to go. As they walked across the room it was quiet, as if it were not the same place that had been blaring with loud music and the shrieks of young girls. After a moment MaDlamini was the first to open her mouth.

'Who the hell does that cripple think he is? C'mon, let's party!' With that she switched the music system on and played it louder than before. She started swinging her arms high from side to side and clicking her fingers. The customers joined her in the dance and the house was filled with jubilation as if there had been no interruption.

Sizwe poured cider into what was supposedly my glass and pushed it to me. 'Drink, my friend,' he said persuasively, 'for beer will get rid of all your sorrows.' But at that moment I was thinking seriously about Skade's statement regarding old man Jongilanga's bereavement. I stood up and headed for the door.

'Hey, Themba. Where do you think you are going?' I heard Sizwe shouting at me.

'To the Apostolic Church. I can't be sitting here when the old man is in trouble.'

'C'mon man, we'll check that one out later.'

'I'm going now. I have no business here!' But before I reached the door I heard MaDlamini screaming at me.

'Hey, where do you think you are going without paying me?'

'What, me paying you? I was only here because Sizwe wanted us to talk. I didn't drink anything.'

'That's not my problem. You bought Sizwe a bottle of Jack Daniels and yourself a Savannah Dry, remember?' she said, opening her hand for me to give her money.

'Sizwe, why did you bring this low-life to my place?'

'Themba, please have a sense of pride, man. Just pay the money before this gets out of hand,' Sizwe persuaded. The conversation was attracting the attention of other customers. I had heard stories about how MaDlamini dealt with male customers who did not want to pay. Legend had it she once pulled a man by his genitals until he told her that he had money in his shoe. She took all the money he had, which was more than he owed her. I was not interested in testing the truth of stories like these.

'Okay, okay, there you go, and keep the change.' I gave her a hundred rand note and left the place immediately. I walked to the Apostolic Church across the street and found the old man still busy cleaning the yard.

'Good afternoon, old man Jongilanga. I came as soon as I got the call. What is wrong, old man? Are you well?'

'My son, you of the majestic clan of AmaMpandla, life is difficult I tell you.'

'Yes, old man. Life is difficult. But are you well?' I was getting exasperated because clearly something was weighing heavily on old man Jongilanga.

'My son, we will say we are well because we wake up and can still put our legs inside our pants. But life is difficult.'

'Ehm, I see old man.' My level of curiosity was subsiding somewhat because old man Jongilanga always preferred to circle round and round like a crow flying in the open skies before attacking a prey on the ground.

'You see me here today because we are about to have a meeting here at the church.'

'I heard about the meeting, but what is the urgent matter?'

'My son, we called an urgent community meeting because I am bereaved.'

'You are bereaved?' The old man confirming the news came to me as a shock because I would have expected to be one of the very first people to be informed when something bad happened to Jongilanga's family. Since my parents had died he had been a father figure to me and I felt compelled to carry out the duties of a son towards him. I wanted to do for the old man what I could not do for my father.

'Yes, my son. Cheetah and Springbok have died.'

'Cheetah and Springbok? Who were they, old man?'

'They were my donkeys, my son.'

'Oh, I see.' I sighed with relief. But despite the fact that it was just donkeys that had died, the old man looked devastated. I reasoned that the seriousness with which he was treating the situation reflected the relative importance of the donkeys to him.

'So, how did they die, old man?'

He took a handkerchief from his pocket and wiped his forehead. 'Come, let's sit down, my son.' He led me inside the church building and we sat in the last row of chairs.

'My son, my donkeys were brutally killed. Somebody shot them.' He stared into space and shook his head in despair.

'Who did that? Why would a reasonable person shoot donkeys?'

'My son, I found my donkeys dead after three days of frantically searching for them. In fact, I would not have found them if it were not for my good neighbour from the AmaTshawe clan.' Jongilanga nervously fumbled for his pipe in his trousers' pockets. Then, probably remembering he was inside the church building, he put the pipe back in his pocket without using it. The church building was probably the only place where the old man did not smoke because he considered it to be a very sacred place.

'Eh, as I was saying, my son,' he continued. 'I looked for my donkeys for three days but could not find them until Tshawe told me that he had seen a donkey standing in the same place for two days below *Intab' Ezono*, the Mountain of Sins.'

I realised that it was very considerate of the old man to have suggested that we sit down because this story was surely going to take a long time to tell. Old man Jongilanga always followed the same formula of storytelling, which included giving a detailed background to the current story.

'I went to look for it, my son, and, as I went down the hill, I saw Cheetah standing motionless by the roadside. I went rushing towards him with excitement. The excitement fizzled out when I started smelling rotten meat as I came close to him. On the other side of the road I saw flies and maggots and the decaying body of Springbok. I also realised that Cheetah had been shot but did not die immediately.

Those who saw him, say that for a day he could move his head around until he stood there motionless. He died standing, my son. That's why we are here.'

Residents were beginning to stream into the church. Among them was the undertaker, Mabelana, who never attended anything unless it was of benefit to him. Perhaps he thought he would be assigned the duty of burying the donkeys since the old man valued them so much.

It was ironic that Skade, the convener of the meeting, was not there yet. In Skade's absence, the old man decided to take the place of chairman and I knew we were going to stay in that room until very late in the evening.

'We are here today because I am bereaved,' old man Jongilanga began the story with his face engulfed with a flush of despair. There were chuckles across the room as he told the residents that he did not know his date of birth, a reason enough for the government to disqualify him for receiving old-age grants.

'The white man in town says I am not eligible for an old-age pension because I do not have a birth certificate. What kind of people are these who do not understand the history that accounts for their presence alongside our people in this land of ours?'

He took a handkerchief to wipe the bald patch on his head. 'My name is Jongilanga, the one who watches the sun. I was named as such because when I was born my mother was still looking over the mountains – from sunset to sunrise, hoping that my father would return from the land of the white man. My father and many other strong men of our people went to assist the white man in fighting other white men during the big war of the world in foreign lands. They never returned because the other white man sank the ship on which they were sailing.'

I found the old man's grasp of history quite fascinating, but as he spoke the corners of his mouth became coated with disgusting foam. I felt like wiping it off for him, but he did not seem to notice at all.

'This happened over a hundred years after the Great War between the Xhosa people and the white man from foreign lands in this land of ours,' he continued. 'That was when our people gave up on the hope for the return of Makana, the great warrior of the Rharhabe who was imprisoned at the island, as they did to Mandela and many other leaders years later.' He went on telling us about the history of the Xhosa people and their confrontations in a series of wars where they were trying to reclaim the land from the European colonisers.

When he was satisfied with the oral history, he began an economics lecture, in which he indicated the importance of the donkeys to him. 'Those with reasonable minds would understand that I was not born yesterday. I have seen well over eighty harvest seasons. No one can employ an old wreck like myself, so these donkeys put food on the table for me. We all want to be as big as Mabelana is: stand up Mabelana so that they can see you . . .'

There were chuckles as the embarrassed Mabelana struggled to get up on his feet. He slowly raised his hand to salute the meeting, his fat cheeks widening as he forced a smile across his face.

'Thank you, Mabelana. You can sit down. I am glad that you have honoured this gathering today. I believe that you are part of the organising committee for the annual Donkey Festival.'

'Yes I am, old man,' Mabelana responded.

'Good, I want you to be part of the delegation that will lead a march to the municipal offices to submit a petition of the donkey owners to the mayor.'

Mabelana got up again to speak, 'Thank you, Mr Chairman. I am humbled by your request, but I beg to decline to be part of the delegation. As a matter of principle, I do not participate in marches.' He sat down promptly.

'What do you mean you don't participate in marches? You are here with us today discussing issues that affect the community. Does this mean you don't support our cause?' old man Jongilanga enquired.

'Not exactly, old man,' Mabelana objected and paused as if gathering strength. 'What I mean is, I don't understand what you expect the mayor to do about stray donkeys that litter our city and fill the roads that are made for our cars? What has to be understood is that Grahamstown is a tourist city. You know that large numbers of tourists stream into our city during the Arts Festival and other occasions. The donkeys should only be allowed in town during the Donkey Festival. That's all that needs to happen.' On that note the old man from the AmaTshawe clan raised his walking stick as an indication that he wanted to speak.

'Okay, let us give the son of the soil – he of the royal blood, a chance to speak. Let the servants keep quiet; the chief is about to speak!' Jongilanga argued.

'Thank you, Jongilanga. The one who watched the sun until it turned into a moon. The one who stands on ostrich legs and touches the Heavens to see where no other man can see.' The man sang praises for old man Jongilanga before he could say what he had stood up to say. 'I stand here to support the motion of marching to the municipality offices. Our demands are clear. We want the mayor and the white man who comes to visit our city to respect us.

Donkeys remain the most accessible mode of transport to the poor masses of this city that they say belongs to the Saints. They also remain a source of income to many like my old friend Jongilanga here,' he said, pointing at old man Jongilanga. 'Our first demand is that there must be a donkey lane on our roads. Secondly, the Donkey Festival must stop being exclusively a tourist attraction event. We must use the festival as a platform to advance the well-being of the poorest of the poor and of the donkeys in this city. Thirdly, we must elect a task team that would draft a petition that would be submitted to the mayor. May I propose that the son of Gwebani be part of the delegation? I want him to use his mighty pen to write down all our demands. Other young activists who would assist him are still out calling people to come to this meeting.'

For a moment I had been deceived into thinking that the old man from the AmaTshawe clan was a sensible being, but then he suggested that I serve on the same committee as Skade. I did not think Skade would want to serve on a committee alongside me either. But then, it is disrespectful to refuse a task that has been bestowed upon you by an elder, especially one of royal blood.

'Will you do that, son of the majestic AmaMpandla clan?'

'Yes, I will, chief of the people,' I agreed, even though inwardly I remained dissatisfied about the arrangement.

'And, Mabelana, we need your help too. Will you offer one of your trucks to take the sick and the elderly to the municipality offices during the march?'

Eh, this is a bit problematic for me. You see, it is not only that I cannot be part of the march; I must not be seen as supporting it as well. The thing is, I also serve on the organising committee of the mayor's Golf Challenge. And, as you know, there we get to rub shoulders with rich cigar-smoking clients – big business people and politicians . . .'

As Mabelana spoke I could not repress my anger at his egocentricity. I stood up and found myself shouting at him, 'Mabelana! Are you sure you belong to this community? Do you know the meaning of the word "sacrifice"

– giving something for a just cause? Will you ever do something out of the goodness of your heart? Mabelana, tell me, have you ever had a baby sleeping in your arms? Have you ever made a baby smile . . .?'

At that moment there was chaos at the church's entrance. The sight that confronted me made me forget about Mabelana. The mayor was being frog-marched in his frog-suit by Skade and a group of young men. It was customary to frog-march men naked when they were found in bed with other men's wives. Everyone knew about this custom, but it had never been verified whether someone who held an esteemed position like the mayor would be treated in the same manner.

'Young man,' old man Jongilanga called to Skade. 'Is this what I think it is?'

'Yes, old man. We found this man in bed with Cirha's wife?' Skade reported.

'Which Cirha are you referring to?' Jongilanga enquired.

'Cirha, the garbage collector, old man.'

'Did you tell Cirha about this?'

'Yes, we called him, old man. But he is scared the mayor will fire him if he confronts him about this incident. He says he can't afford to lose his job over a loose-thighed woman.'

'And where is the wife now?' old man Jongilanga enquired.

'She is standing naked in front of other married women who are executing the punishment for her shameful deed.'

Old man Jongilanga looked circumspectly at the naked mayor. After a while he turned to the people and remarked, 'Now what is going on in our society? What can we do when a man is scared of an adulterer – a man who's been found in bed with his wife?'

'Let's kill the bastard!' Skade shouted.

'We cannot bathe the house of God with the sinner's blood. Remember the saying, "violence begets violence",' responded Jongilanga. 'This incident further validates our cause. We cannot be led by such a disgraced individual whose genitals have been touched by every other woman in this community.'

The old man from the AmaTshawe clan rose to his feet without having raised his hand to show that he had something to say. 'Jongilanga, my age-mate, our custom allows us to deal with an adulterer in a way that would discourage any other man to commit a similar offence. Now, if we act according to our customary law the white man's law would label us as lawless vigilantes.'

As he spoke, the elder from the AmaTshawe clan walked slowly towards the podium and stood next to the naked mayor. While we were still listening to the old man's narrative with interest, we heard a deep bellow of agony from the mayor. The old man had pointed with his walking stick and then mustered all his strength to unleash a vicious blow across the mayor's naked back. A brown body fled from the church building with several hands smacking him as he went past. The mayor ran so fast that he did not seem to feel his big round belly that hung in front of him like a sack of maize. A few like old man Jongilanga tried to mediate, urging people not to take the law into their own hands. For a while there was chaos until old man Jongilanga persuaded everyone to go back to their seats.

'That's how you deal with an adulterer. He should be grateful that we cannot remove his troublesome testicles for him,' the elder from the AmaTshawe clan remarked with great fury. 'If the white man thinks our practices are inappropriate, he should let me sleep with his wife and we will see how he would react.' By this time the old man's blood was clearly boiling. 'I am of royal blood; it is my duty to ensure that our people keep all cultural practices that remain relevant to our present day lives. Even the head of government sitting in the white man's house in the big city recognises our role as traditional leaders.' With that, he took the coat that he had draped on his chair and walked slowly towards the door.

'My people, our soil needs some cleansing. The son of the soil is not happy. The people of Makana are not happy. God is not happy. We have now upset the Creator by behaving violently in his house,' old man Jongilanga began to lament the recent incident and the moral decadence that afflicted our society.

After the old man had spoken, the task team, which I was part of, was entrusted with drafting a memorandum demanding the establishment of a donkey lane and the immediate removal of the mayor. I supported the cause, but I did not imagine myself working amicably with Skade. I had forced myself to attend this meeting knowing that Skade would be there, but I did not think he would be too pleased with the idea of working closely with me either. As I left the meeting I was still debating the situation in my mind.

14

A man enslaved

The silence of my empty house had become too loud. It was only interrupted by unwarranted visits from curious neighbours, which rubbed salt into the already unbearable wound of becoming a public villain. The visits were constant reminders of the misery that had wrecked my life. Without my wife and children, my house had become a hollow cave that resounded with agonising echoes with every beat of my heart.

When I did venture out of the house people looked at me in a way that made me feel like I was a different species. I was so ostracised by the community that even those who knew me would look in the other direction when they came across me, as if I had a contagious disease that they could contract even by breathing the same air as me. I realised with horror that the community saw me as an incarnation of a monster that threatened to swallow every being within its reach. The neighbours' children were strictly warned to stay away from me. All of this forced me to live a reclusive life.

My withdrawal from society helped me to avoid hearing things that would only cause further destruction in my life. I know it sounds absurd, but at times it's good not to know. What you don't know cannot hurt you. Ignorance can be a form of wisdom.

My manhood was overwhelmed with fear – the fear of knowing. I feared knowing that I might have contracted a deadly virus from my rendezvous with Nosipho. It hurt when I heard that Nosipho was dying. The fact that she had disclosed her sickness to the entire community was an assault on my conscience. The reality that the virus that was reducing her to a wasted skeleton could have been circulating in my blood as well was an excruciating realisation.

Nosipho had sent several messages that she wanted to see me before her soul departed. I wanted to see her too. I wanted to know how she had got the virus. I wanted to know when she became aware of her sickness. I wanted to hear that she did not have the virus before I slept with her. I wanted to hear that I didn't have HIV in my blood. But I didn't want anyone to see me talking to Nosipho. Her public disclosure about the sickness was indicative of her courage and determination to spread knowledge about the disease and eradicate the stigma that it carried.

'Knock knock, is there anyone in here?' It was old man Jongilanga. He was already inside. I hadn't heard him open the door.

'Come in, have a seat, old man,' I said, ushering him to the sofa.

'Old man, how long have you been standing here?' I asked, wondering if he had noticed that my mind was elsewhere.

'Long enough to see that something is really eating the young man,' he said, putting his walking stick on the floor.

'Nothing much, old man. I was just, I was just thinking about my children.'

Old man Jongilanga was the last man I intended sharing my problems with. I knew a conversation with him would open the floodgates of morality lessons.

'Well, thinking alone is not very good, my son. You've got to share your problems otherwise we'll find your cold body dangling from the ceiling of this house. That is why God created a woman, to be on your side in times of joy and of trouble.' He started with his sermons, but today I wasn't in the mood to listen to them.

'Thanks for the lesson, old man. Now, what can I help you with?' I couldn't help showing my annoyance. So many people had come to my house with the intention of 'reasoning' with me but I was not interested in listening to people who did not know what they were talking about. What bothered me most was that they all talked as if it was my choice to have my family flee from me.

'Son of Gwebani, I have seen many suns, but the happenings of today are far beyond my wisdom. Where have you ever seen rabbits chasing dogs, rats attacking cats?' He paused briefly to light his pipe. Old man Jongilanga was the only person allowed to smoke in my house. In fact, because he was a father figure to me he did not need to ask for my permission. 'That is what is happening today, my son. Children are dying before their parents. Many of my age-mates are becoming parents to their grandchildren. Son of the AmaMpandla clan, are we a cursed people that young people continue to perish like flies? Who will build this society when everyone falls victim to this *big fever*?'

'Old man, isn't it the doctors you should be talking to? I for one cannot do anything to stop the disease.' This conversation was really getting on my nerves, but as an elder old man Jongilanga was still eligible to a certain portion of respect.

'My son, maybe you think there is nothing you can do because you do not have medical expertise, but believe me, there is so much you can do for this community.' He blew a cloud of smoke through his mouth.

'Old man, I think you are talking to the wrong person. I have been stripped of my portfolio as a community leader and a principal. Why don't you speak to the mayor?' I was still trying to overcome the humiliation I had caused myself through my actions, which left me at the lowest levels of moral decadence in our community.

'Son of my age-mate, this is not about leadership. There is a young girl who would like to talk to you before she dies. I know that she has been sending messages to you but you keep ignoring them. I decided to come myself and hear from you why you do not want to relieve this girl from the sufferings of this world. The gods have sustained her soul until she meets you. And if she dies without speaking to you that would bring misfortune to your house.'

Our people are so paranoid about bad fortune. Sometimes they go through so much suffering just to avoid misfortune that might or might not occur.

'Old man Jongilanga, there can never be any worse misfortune than what I have been through. I was once a respected man in the society and look, now I'm just a shadow of the man I used to be.'

'Son of my age-mate, what you are experiencing is only . . .'

'Old man,' I interrupted, 'what's the worst that could happen to a man? Let me ask you, perhaps you'll have an idea: has your wife ever run away from you; did your children ever refuse to come to you; did they look at you like you were a monster?'

'No, no, my son, but . . .'

'Exactly! You know nothing about what I'm going through so don't try to convince me that it's nothing. I need to pull myself out of this rut first before being a Messiah to strangers. So please act on my behalf and take whatever message she wants to deliver to me.' I was growing increasingly furious and my respect for the old man had faded away.

'Son of AmaMpandla clan,' the light in his pipe had died down but old man Jongilanga continued inhaling anyhow, 'that girl is on her deathbed. She will be joining the living dead soon. You must never dare disrespect the dead and the dying. For if they forsake you, you will be embroiled in eternal misfortune.'

'Thank you, old man Jongilanga. That makes me feel much better,' I said, and stood up to open the door for him. 'Please close the gate on your way out.'

The old man looked at me for a while without uttering a word. He shook his head and fumbled for his walking stick. As he walked out the door he turned to look at me with eyes that were overcast with distress.

'You had better be careful, my son. You had better be careful,' he said, and walked away as fast as he could.

Old man Jongilanga's departure ushered in an even more agonising silence.

I sat there with no one to talk to, no one to share my frustrations with, or even to take them out on. I was alone. I was a free man and yet I felt so constrained. I had become a prisoner in my own house. Memory became a gruesome monster in me as it brought back all the pain that had become prevalent in my being. I was engulfed with a feeling of regret, but what has been done cannot be undone. As my mind went back and forth, it dawned on me that I had not treated old man Jongilanga with the dignity he deserved as an elder. At least there was still a chance to rectify my mistake with him. A wise man knows when to compromise. I would repent, but there was no undoing what had happened between Nosipho and me. It was deeply embedded in my consciousness. How do I break the emotional shackles of my being, of my manhood? How do I erase the shameful trajectory that trails behind me? How do I evade the sorry image that I have created for myself in the face of the unforgiving community of Sekunjalo?

When I looked at the time I realised that it was barely two hours after old man Jongilanga had left. I decided to go and find him to apologise; maybe he would understand. But first I had to take a bath. In the last few days I had not bothered to keep myself clean because I had not interacted with other people anyway. My freedom was viciously enslaving. Now I had taken the decision to go and apologise to old man Jongilanga for my utterances earlier in the day. I knew he had no room for malevolence in his heart, not for a very long time at least. While I was still in the bath there was another knock at the door.

'*Ungubani?*' I wanted to know who it was before bothering to come out of the bath unnecessarily.

'It's me, my son.' I recognised old man Jongilanga's voice. I immediately got out of the bath and wrapped a towel around my waist. I knew he might have come to look for his pipe, which I was sure he had taken with him when he left. He had done that many times before. When we were young boys he had once accused us of playing a trick with him by hiding his pipe. We looked all over and after a while I noticed that it was in his mouth. He was a very wise man but forgetfulness was taking its toll on him as he got older. I was hoping that he had forgotten all that had happened during his visit earlier in the day. Perhaps the gods of my people had decided to bring him back so that I could ask for forgiveness before it was too late.

'Old man, it's wonderful to have you back,' I said as a sign of warm welcome.

'I wish I could say the same, my son,' he said, wiping his forehead with a handkerchief. I recognised the gesture as a sign of exasperation from the old man.

'Why are you talking like that now, old man?' I was concerned because I found his mood strikingly different from his earlier visit.

'Son of Gwebani, you see me here because I am from that home. Even before I told the girl that you could not see her, she told me she already knew what you had said to me. She then asked me to tell you that her soul will not rest in peace unless you speak at her funeral. That was her last wish, and those were the last words that came out of her mouth. Then she closed her eyes and slept an eternal sleep.'

'Old man, you mean she died?' I said with astonishment.

'I believe that her body had long ceased to exist. It was only her soul that remained. Now even her soul has departed, but I believe that she continues to exist among the living dead.'

'What else did she tell you, old man? Please tell me, what else? Did she say anything about how she got the disease?'

'No, my son, nothing of a profound nature that I can recall. Only her grandmother said something that left me bewildered.' He paused briefly and cleared his throat, 'I don't know how to put this, my son. My body is still shivering.'

'Don't be nervous, old man. Just tell me, what did she say?' It was clear that old man Jongilanga was the bearer of bad news, but I was eager to hear his words anyway.

'My son, that woman told me that Nosipho was not really her son's daughter.'

'Yes, old man,' I said, nodding my head to encourage him to go on.

'That girl was very strong; she had been lying in that bed for a very long time. She was brave to talk about the disease. My son, that girl had a big heart; she had the power to skin a leopard alive, a feat that is known only among your clan,' he explained.

'What do you mean, old man?' I was utterly bewildered.

'My son, that girl was born in prison fifteen years ago. She comes from your Aunt Gladys's womb. Your aunt was believed to have been impregnated by the man who killed your uncle. But that girl has the blood of the AmaMpandla clan, my son.'

'Old man, please speak simple language to me. I don't understand what you are trying to say.' I did not know what to make of what the old man was saying. Perhaps I understood, but I wished he were wrong.

'That girl has your blood, my son,' he said simply.

Suddenly it dawned on me that Nosipho had been born in the same year that Aunt Gladys was imprisoned. That was a few months after I found myself in bed with her. Could it be possible that I had got Aunt Gladys pregnant? Could it be possible that Nosipho was my daughter? Could it be possible that I had penetrated my own daughter's girlhood?

'Son, are you still with me?' Old man Jongilanga's voice seemed to be echoing from a distance.

'Actually, I don't know, old man. I feel like I don't know anything about myself. What kind of a man am I? I did not recognise the product of my own seed.' I was suddenly engulfed with a great feeling of regret.

'These things happen, my son,' he tried to comfort me.

'But why do they have to happen to me all the time? Maybe I deserve this, old man. After all I was never wanted. I was cursed before I was born.' What pained me most was that it was clear that I had rubbed all my misfortunes onto my offspring. Coming from my seed was a curse to Nosipho's entire life.

I wanted to cry like a bereaved woman. But I am a man. A man never cries. He bows his head and listens to the pain deep inside him. The making of a man is the ability to contain tears even when they try to force their way out.

15

A man reborn

As I am sitting on the couch I hear what sounds like a growling dog, accompanied by the whining sounds of puppies. No barking. I get up and open the door to see what is causing the irritating sound. There is the Sekunjalo bitch on my lawn.

The dog is one of the most famous 'animal legends' in Sekunjalo. No one knows who its owner is or where it comes from. But everyone knows about it. Some claim that the bitch possesses potent venom, so that a bite from her could send a man to the ranks of his ancestors. I have seen the bitch upsetting rubbish bins and feeding on the human excrement that fills the buckets left waiting on the roadside to be collected by the refuse truck. Rumours have been doing the rounds that the bitch turns into a baboon at night and the owner, who is said to be one of the elderly women in the community, rides on its back when performing her sorcery. The Great Witch, as she is widely known, apparently rides it facing backwards, though no one claims to have seen it happen.

Then there is Bushie the goat. Bushie is as tall as a grown calf and his spiral horns resemble those of his cousin in the wild – the kudu. He is known to drink beer with men at shebeens and when there is a traditional ceremony. On several occasions I have seen Bushie helping himself to cabbages on the vegetable stands of street vendors. One has to be careful when attempting to discipline Bushie; he can be very aggressive at times. A man who once tried to chase Bushie away from his garden found himself shielding Bushie with one hand and trying to cover his buttocks with the other after Bushie had torn the man's pants with his strong horns. When he realised that the goat was gaining the upper hand, the man took to his heels with Bushie in hot pursuit.

And then there is the Brahman ox. The ox belonged to the late Qhinebe, himself a legendary figure in the vicinity of Makana. There are several versions of the story about the ox and its significance in the community. The version that seems most logical to me is that the ox was Qhinebe's favourite bull. It was very generous in implanting its semen and mated with several cows, which were predominantly jersey cows. The community started complaining because the jerseys were breeding Brahman cows, and Brahmans are not good milk producers, which is one of the most critical resources in the community. The bull was castrated and it became a very aggressive beast. Some claimed that Qhinebe was happy about the aggressiveness of the beast because the castration of the bull was done against his will. As he put it, he wanted his bull to enjoy all the benefits of his masculinity.

'No woman was present when my bull was castrated. I wonder what those men would say if I were to remove their testicles as they did to my bull,' old man Qhinebe had argued in a community meeting where he lodged a complaint about the castration of his bull. Nevertheless, the Brahman bull, which had now been turned into an ox, was seen as a threat to the community. A few days after this meeting, old man Qhinebe died quietly in his sleep. His clansmen decided that they would slaughter his favourite ox as a sacrifice to send him to the land of the living dead. As men surrounded the ox in order to tie it up for slaughtering, the ox began to walk around the cattle enclosure breathing heavily. Mbatyothi, an expert in tying the most unruly oxen, came towards the beast whistling and singing praises for it to remain calm. The ox stood motionless and fixed its eyes on Mbatyothi. Just when everybody was beginning to think that Mbatyothi had tamed the aggressive beast, it suddenly charged at him. In the blink of an eye Mbatyothi was on the ground with a gaping wound in his side. Other men saw the anger in the beast's eyes and

immediately ran for safety with the beast on their heels. The ox charged out
of the enclosure and never went back. Now it lives almost as a wild animal,
without a home, without an owner.

These are the stories of Sekunjalo. No one cares about recording them. We
just live with them and they are passed from generation to generation through
word of mouth. No one questions their validity or challenges their logic. We
were brought up in a tradition of not questioning norms and beliefs. I had to
believe in or do things in a particular way because they were done that way
by my parents and their parents before them. My parents were part of the
community and observed its norms and values.

One of the beliefs was that you dare not challenge the evil unless you had
been cleansed by a strong diviner. This is probably why people are quite
loath to attack the bitch, despite the fact that everyone wants her dead.

I look around for a stone to chase it away from my lawn, but my yard is
too clean to find a stone lying around. I come closer to the bitch and its
bloodshot eyes meet mine. It does not run away as I would expect a dog to
do. I see in its mouth what looks like a puppy – presumably its own puppy.
The growling is much deeper than I had heard earlier. It's a very aggressive
growl – almost as loud as a lion's. Blood is dripping from the corners of its
mouth as it dips its canines into the flesh of the puppy. The growling is becoming
more aggressive and the anger is clearly directed towards me. The dog leaves
its breakfast and charges at me. I make an about turn to run for safety and I
find a deep hole behind me. I fall and fall into the hole . . .

I see stars flying all over as I hit my forehead on the floor. It's a dream! I've
been dreaming but it's real that I hit my forehead against the floor as I fell
from the couch where I was sleeping. I look at my watch. It is four twenty-

five in the morning. Today is Sunday, the first day of August 2004. It is Lammas day. The day that my prodigal daughter will be buried. Was she a prodigal daughter or I have been a prodigal father throughout her living days? Whichever way you choose to look at it, the reality is that Nosipho was a product of my seed and now she is dead.

My neck hurts, probably from my uncomfortable sleep on the couch. I go to the bedroom and take my shoes off but leave my pants on. It's already morning; there's no point in trying to catch up on some sleep. I lie on top of the blankets and the thought of Nosipho creeps in again. I don't want to think about her. What is the point of thinking when there is no solution? Nosipho is dead and I never had a chance to give her the love of a father. My watch says it's four thirty-nine and I think it is too slow. I can't wait until it's morning, but I'm not looking forward to the day. The day of my daughter's burial – a ceremony that I am not going to attend. Today the community of Sekunjalo will be saying 'earth to earth' and 'dust to dust' to my daughter's remains. I can't sleep. I look at the time again and now it's four fifty. I don't know how I'm going to get through this horrendous day. Suddenly I hear what sounds like a falling object outside my house and I go to open the front door to check on the noise.

As I step outside I find the Sekunjalo bitch in the corner of my well-fenced yard. It is helping itself to the contents of the rubbish bin. Rubbish is now scattered all over my yard. I give my thigh a pinch to make sure I am not dreaming. I feel the pinch and I can see the dog is very much alive as it looks at me and tucks its tail between its hind legs with fear. I've heard stories about the bitch, and it has continued to haunt me even in my dreams. I am not prepared to take chances with it. I am reluctant to go back inside the house to look for a weapon to chase it away lest it should pounce on me whilst I have my back turned. I find myself standing motionless and the bitch looks at me without moving. This must be the proverbial mad dog because a normal dog would either run away or growl at the person who seems to be a threat to it. After a while the bitch decides to ignore me and hesitantly continues upsetting my rubbish bin in search of food. Its long breasts are dangling and its ribs are clearly visible under its skin as it balances on the rubbish bin with its front legs.

I feel a twinge of sympathy for the hungry dog. Perhaps it's because now I can relate to her situation. The bitch has been living as an outcast in society and if it were not for the often irritating visits by the likes of old man Jongilanga, I would be akin to a hermit by now. It is well known that since my family turned their backs on me I have lived a somewhat reclusive life. I am not exactly a hermit, but a close cousin to it. There is nothing reprehensible about a human hermit assisting a dog hermit.

I return to the house to check if I can give her some crumbs and bones from the food and takeaways that I ate yesterday. I scrape out the remains of the porridge from the pot and mix them with the bones that I find in a KFC box. I go to give the food to the malnourished bitch so that she can eat and leave my place. But I find her already standing in the doorway as if she knew I was collecting some food for her. I do not have a dish for the dog so I spill the food on the floor and the bitch readily cleans it with her tongue. Part of the food falls onto my feet and the tongue starts licking the porridge from my toes in the sandals that I am wearing. I feel her tongue rubbing on my skin and it tickles. For the first time in a very long time I find myself laughing. I go back to the kitchen and put the now almost clean pot in the kitchen sink.

I come back to the sitting room and find the dog lying flat with her belly on the floor rug. She wags her tail as I appear from the kitchen. I feel good that some creature out there is happy to see me, appreciates who I am; and is able to make me laugh. I sit on the floor next to the bitch. I lie with my belly on the floor and rest my chin on my right fist. I stretch out my left hand and reach for the body of the bitch. I start cuddling her silky body. I am lying next to one of the most famous and feared figures in Sekunjalo and yet I don't have the fright that I used to have when I heard people talking about the deadly venom of the bitch. The bitch is known all over the township, but I never heard anyone calling her by her name. They all call her, excuse me, we all used to call her 'the bitch', but today I am going to give her a new name. Her name is Lily. She's like that beautiful plant that grows in the most awkward of places, river banks and all. Yes, 'Lily' is the right name for her. She also has a healing power, just as the leaves of the lily are used to cure septic wounds and insect bites.

Lily closes her eyes as I continue caressing her silky soft body. I come closer to her face and she seems unfazed by my closeness to her. I come closer and touch my nose with hers. Her body is warm but her nose is as cold as ice. She opens her eyes slightly and releases a pleasant whine that sounds like 'I do'. I try to draw her closer to me but her body will not roll towards me. I look at her breasts and notice that there are fleas all over her belly and body. I look around and see fleas on the floor rug and when I look at my clothes I realise they are walking all over me too. I begin to feel them feeding on my blood and my whole body gets itchy. I jump up immediately and head for the shower, leaving Lily in the sitting room.

I take my clothes off and open the cold tap. I like cold water at times like these because it refreshes my mind and perhaps my soul as well. As I stand naked in the shower with cold water running down my body, I look at my shrunken penis. It's much smaller than usual. It is such a small part of my body, but ironically it is the reason I find myself in all the troubles that I am embroiled in today.

My mind takes me back over my long history of sexual associations and I wonder about what they have earned me. I was pushed into resigning and thus was stripped of my portfolio as a councillor; I was dismissed as the acting principal of Sinethemba High School. All because of a moment's pleasure.

Was there pleasure or was it just satisfaction – satisfaction that I had managed to add another woman to my long list of sexual victims? Is there satisfaction when you make love hurriedly in fear of getting caught? Perhaps satisfaction is not the right word. What about pride? Is there pride when you triumph over a helpless soul? Did making love to a girl as young as fifteen make me a better man? Was it lovemaking or was it just sexual intercourse? I don't remember kissing Nosipho. What is sex without a kiss? Is it possible to make love without loving?

I have a long record of dealings with women but these are questions that I still cannot answer. And my actions have had consequences that will haunt me to the grave.

I switch off the tap and take a towel to dry my body. I check the time again; it's five forty-one, and I'm happy that a few minutes have passed without noticing. The shower seemed to do the trick. Now that my main activity for the day is done, I go back to the sitting room. Lily is not where I left her. I look under the coffee table and she is not there. I look under my bed and she is not there either. I find myself screaming 'Lily', but there is no answer. I realise that she will not know her name as yet. I imagine that she may not have known that I was taking a shower and may have thought that I was abandoning her. Because getting rid of the fleas and my accumulated dirt was an emergency I could not indicate to her that I would be back. Now she is out there with dogs that will father her babies and leave her to raise fatherless puppies. Irresponsible bastards!

In a flash of honest self-awareness I know that today I am perceived by some as one of those bastards who litter the surface of the Earth with their offspring and never take full responsibility. I am here today, in what is supposed to be a family home. This space feels like a big four-roomed cave. My children are not here. My wife is not here. Even Lily has deserted me.

Unbidden, the thought comes to me again: today is Sunday the first of August, the day that the remains of my daughter will be laid to rest. I cannot bear the thought any longer. I look for my keys. They are not in my trousers' pockets. They are not on the couch either. I go to the bedroom and look inside the drawer but they are not there. Forget about them, I tell myself. I'll leave the house unlocked. After all, I've lost all the important assets in my life. My wife left me. My children followed their mother. Nosipho is dead. And now Lily has deserted me.

As I close the door, I find my bunch of keys dangling in the keyhole. I must have left them here yesterday. I lock the door and walk away.

The sun has not risen yet. In fact, it does not seem like it will be a bright day. The sky is overcast and a cold wind is lightly shaking the trees.

I keep walking until I reach Skade's shack. There is a long and deep trench that runs in front of his door into another yard. I take it as a good sign that soon there will be running water in the settlement.

I notice the door which is being used across the trench as a bridge to Skade's shack. It is green and is inscribed S.H.S. with white paint. The abbreviations stand for Sinethemba High School, which means that someone has vandalised the school. I decide to ignore it and walk across the door-bridge to Skade's shack. I knock but there is no answer. I knock again. Quiet. I knock again harder than before.

'Who is it?' a voice says from inside.

'It's me,' I respond.

'Who is "me"? Don't you have a name?' he asks irritably.

'It's me, Themba, Themba Limba.' There is a brief pause.

'Oh, why didn't you say? Just saying it's me, it's me.' I hear him mumbling as he walks towards the door. The door knob turns from the inside and the door opens. Skade emerges from behind the door with bleary half-open eyes. His face is not washed. I haven't seen him like this since we were boys, the only difference now is that his face is full of wrinkles and he has grown some whiskers.

'Now, why do you knock on my door like a policeman?'

'I'm sorry, man. I thought you were sleeping.'

'Of course I was sleeping. You had better have a good reason for disturbing my sleep,' he says, turning without inviting me in. The stump of his leg jiggles freely as he hops around on one leg. The sight of him jumping back to the bed on one leg is irrepressibly comical and I find myself smiling. I see his artificial leg naked for the first time as it rests against the wall. He goes on mumbling, 'I value my sleep. We never slept much in the forests while the likes of you were lying comfortably in your beds at university.'

'No man, I just need, I just need a haircut.'

'What? You wake me up at six in the morning to tell me that you want a haircut? Are you out of your mind?'

'Yes . . . no . . . I'm sorry, man. It's just that I could not sleep.'

'Man, you had better have something better to say. I don't have time for this nonsense. Besides, why would you let me cut your hair because you know I hate your guts?'

Despite his tough words I suddenly get a feeling that he is prepared to reconcile with me. I know that deep down in his heart he does not despise me as much as other people seem to think he does. Skade is the kind of man who likes to appear rough, but he is very soft inside.

'Skade, listen! I'm sorry, man.' I am prepared to drop my pride for the sake of making up. I say these words while boldly looking him in the eyes.

'Sorry for what?' he asks triumphantly, and I can see he is enjoying this encounter.

'After all these years, I have realised that the differences between us are not worth sacrificing our friendship.'

'Look here, Themba, you should have thought about our friendship before turning out to be an *impimpi*.'

'I've never been an informer!' I am aware that he has been spreading rumours that I was on the side of the enemy during the movement days. It is true that I was never arrested and never suffered any permanent physical injuries. But what he seems to overlook is that under apartheid as long as you were a black man you were oppressed.

'Never? Then why is your aunt in prison? Heh, didn't you inform the police about some comrades' underground movements which your uncle was a victim of?'

I feel like I am standing in some kangaroo court trying to mend our broken camaraderie.

'There was no underground movement. I informed the police because Aunt Gladys, together with that man, plotted and killed my uncle. That's criminal.'

For a long time black people had viewed the state police as enemies and confused some criminal acts with the actions of the struggle. In some cases this is why our people are still reluctant to report criminal cases to the police.

'Maybe that is partly criminal, but it doesn't excuse the fact that you humiliated me in a community meeting.'

'Forget about that, man. You probably got the position after I was sacked anyhow,' I say, trying to console him.

'I never got the position. That round-bellied mayor gave it to his mistress,' he says with obvious resentment.

'Which mistress is that now?' I ask with shock.

'The very same girl you fought over.'

'Dolly? Dolly is now the councillor for this community? You must be joking!'

'I'm telling you. Now that girl is the representative of Sekunjalo though she does not know a thing about this community. All in the name of Affirmative Action.'

'Oh, man, I should've known,' I say. While I had been a councillor I had made a point of ensuring that there was transparency in job appointments, which made it impossible for the mayor to create a position for Dolly in the office. Now he had used his power to make a ruling over the appointment of a so called caretaker councillor.

Skade tries to fix his artificial leg and I pretend not to notice because he seems embarrassed. He sits on his bed, which is now shaped somewhat like a ship – high on both ends and the middle so low it is almost touching the ground. It has definitely served its time, I observe to myself.

'Okay, come!' He walks outside his shack with electric clippers in his hand. I wonder why we have to go outside, but I follow him anyway. He is the boss now. He takes a municipality-provided rubbish bin and empties it into a black rubbish bag. I wonder where he got the rubbish bin from because the informal part of Sekunjalo is not eligible to have these bins. He ties the plastic bag and hangs it on a tree next to his house.

'What are you hanging it there for?' I ask just to make him feel good. I know what a delight it will be to Skade when I seem naive and he appears as the one with knowledge.

'You, you are educated for nothing. You are not a strategist,' he says. 'Can't you see that it's for the dogs?'

'What about the dogs?' I ask with disdain.

'If I leave the plastic bag here dogs will rip it and the rubbish will fly all over the place. I'm being environmentally responsible.'

'Oh, I see. I didn't think about it,' I find myself saying.

'Sit here!' He instructs me to sit on the bottom of the rubbish bin which he has now turned upside down. Clearly he is enjoying our interaction.

Skade pulls out electric wires from where the rubbish bin was sitting. He connects the ends of the power cord of the electric clippers to the wires. The connection has been made illegally from my section of the township across the road, which means that I pay for the electricity used by Skade and his neighbours in the settlement. The settlement is host to a multitude of electrical engineers who never went through formal schooling to acquire their expertise. Many of them have died in the line of duty after being shocked by failed connections.

'So, that's how you get electricity?' I find myself saying.

'Where did you think we got it from? You know we are struggling in this settlement,' he responds, and I realise that I had never bothered to find out how Skade and the rest of the shack dwellers got electricity.

'While you people shit in toilets inside your houses in your area we still shit in buckets in the cold outside.'

'C'mon, Skade. You don't need to be that mean.' I had heard enough of these complaints from the residents during my tenure as a councillor and I am not interested in hearing them again.

'What do you mean I'm being mean? All you guys know with that mayor of yours is how to embezzle municipality funds with all the pretty women in this township.' He talks with his usual emphasis on words, as if he is addressing a crowd.

'But at least there is progress. I see that there are trenches, which is a good sign that there will be running water soon.'

'Trenches? Are you talking about these trenches that make it hard for us to walk around our township? I thought now that you were getting your senses back you'd be able to think logically.'

'You mean what I'm saying is not reasonable?'

'You still ask? Those trenches were dug just after you left the municipality and they have remained like this since. You know what that was done for?'

'To keep people's hopes high,' I say, feeling happy that I can contribute to Skade's argument.

'To prevent people from calling for your reinstatement after he replaced you with that girl. They will dig more trenches when voting time is near to make sure they get support from the people. You need to be a lateral thinker to understand these things.'

'Oh, I see,' I say.

'Okay, forget about that. How do you want me to cut your hair?' Now we are back to business – what brought me here in the first place.

'Shave all of it off as is done at times of bereavement.'

'C'mon, man, what are you cutting all your hair for?' he asks with astonishment.

'I'm cutting my hair in accordance with the custom of my people at times of bereavement,' I say sternly.

'So, who are you mourning, if I may ask?'

'My daughter.'

'Which daughter? I saw your two girls with your wife just yesterday.'

'No, not one of them. Today is Nosipho's funeral.'

'I know about Nosipho, but what's your relationship with her?' Skade asks with bewilderment.

'Nosipho was my daughter.'

'You must be running mad, man.'

'Nosipho was my daughter. I didn't know until the time of her death.'

'Man, you mean . . . I mean, eh . . .' he stammers with shock.

'Yes, I slept with my aunt exactly fifteen years ago. Nosipho was the product of that encounter.' I feel relieved to talk about this rendezvous to someone. I've been keeping it to myself for a very long time.

'Man, I can't believe this.'

'Yeah, I couldn't believe it myself.'

'Okay, sit here, let me clean the clippers,' he says, and runs the shoe brush over the blades of the clippers. He blows the clippers and holds it against the sun. He takes what used to be a white cloth and wipes the blades with it.

'So, how was Dolly elected to take my place?' I am trying to ease the tension.

'There was no election. The mayor said he was gonna use his powers to fill the gap. He said it was too late for the community to look for a new candidate.'

'Ag, that scoundrel. He always manipulates the system to his benefit.' I am glad that we have a common enemy.

'That man will always get what he wants as long as he still occupies that position. Can you believe that he got away with the adultery case by promoting the garbage collector to the position of a tractor driver?' Skade says with obvious resentment.

'He won't always win,' I say wishfully. 'By the way, when is the march?'

'During the Donkey Festival in August. It's just over two weeks away. But we will remove BV from office, believe me. I have built a strong case against him. He has sexually harassed half the women in that municipality,' Skade says confidently.

'It's been pretty much obvious. But who'll testify against him?' I enquire because I also know that the mayor has his ways of silencing people although I don't have tangible evidence for this.

'We have at least three reliable witnesses. Your lady friend, Dolly, is one of them. And it's likely that more will come forward once action is taken against him.'

I nod in agreement and Skade holds my forehead so that it remains still. I hold up my hand signalling him to stop.

'What is it now? Do you want me to cut your hair or not?' Skade asks irritably.

'*Ja*, but tell me. What's your succession plan?'

'What?' I sense that he has not given this matter serious thought.

'Your succession plan. Who do you think can succeed BV?' I try to simplify the question.

'You know, I haven't really thought about it. But now that you mention it, I think Miss Phatheka could be a good candidate, although on a personal level she can make some really bad choices.'

I feel my heart beating heavily against my chest. 'Okay, you can carry on,' I say. This feels too personal because everyone thinks that Miss Phatheka's worst decision was falling in love with my brother, Zakes.

He starts cutting my hair and we don't say much to each other. He holds me by the chin and turns my head this way and that. He stands from a distance like a surveyor observing a landscape. He comes back and carefully runs his clippers on my scalp.

'But I thought you were supposed to make it bald,' I say, trying to tell him that he does not need to demonstrate his surveying skills on my head.

'Of course I'm removing all your hair, but even that requires skill.'

I don't comment any further. I let Skade 'The Artist' do whatever he wants with my head. I recall that he was rumoured to be an aspirant writer.

'I hear that you have taken up writing. What made you take that up?' I try to raise a topic that I know will excite him.

'It's all about setting the record straight. I am tired of reading stories that I cannot relate to. I want to tell the story of my people as I know it first hand,' he argues somewhat boastfully.

'I see. How's it coming along? Someone said you've written about seven stories.'

'No, I've been writing the same story seven times. I never get to finish it.'

There is frustration in Skade's voice and I decide to keep my mouth shut and let him do his job. After what seems like an eternity I hear him say, 'Finished.' He dusts his machine with a white handkerchief.

'Really?' I say, and touch my head from the back, running my hand through to the front. I do that instinctively each time I get my hair cut. I see my hair on the floor and I am amazed that I had that much hair on my head. I take out a twenty rand note and give it to him.

'Thank you, man,' he says, and puts it in his trousers' pocket. He collects my hair from the floor and rolls it into a bundle. Then he wraps it in a piece of paper and prepares to burn it.

16

When a man cries

I watch Skade burning my hair behind his shack. The fire has a somewhat bluish flame and the smell of burned hair reminds me of the death of my parents. Their bodies were burned to ashes but they still occupy a large space in my mind. Their lives were cut short as Skade has done to my hair. My hair is burned. Part of me is destroyed. But hair, unlike flesh, will grow again. Perhaps I will grow new hair with patches of grey because I am not growing any younger. So many things have happened in my life – things that cannot be reversed. Many of these experiences, the good and the bad, remain in my memory. I realise that in these last few months I have learned from them and now I hope to live my life differently.

Why do bad memories seem to linger above all others? I ask myself. I don't know the answer. Skade probably wouldn't know the answer either. I decide to leave.

'Where are you going?' Skade asks with great concern. Because I came to apologise to him he now seems to feel some responsibility for my life, so much so that he has appointed himself as my guardian. I decide not to say this to Skade, in accordance with my people's proverb, 'Never forget the honey bird'. Skade has been good to me lately and, in a sense, he is the proverbial honey bird. I don't want to upset him lest I damage our new camaraderie – and at the moment I don't have too many friends to speak of.

'To the funeral,' I say heavily. I had responded without thinking, but now there's no swallowing my words.

'Are you sure?' There is obvious hesitation in Skade's question. In actual fact, I am not sure if I should attend the funeral, but there is no changing my mind now.

'I'm positive!' I say to him emphatically so that he does not doubt my integrity and ability to keep my word.

'Wait, I'll come with you,' he says, and puts on his black jacket. He takes his old school blazer and hands it to me.

'Here, wear this.' It dawns on me that one is supposed to wear a jacket when attending a funeral service. I put on Skade's blazer and leave while Skade is fumbling to lock his shack. I am already on the street and can hear Skade's footsteps drawing closer as he tries to catch up with me.

The sky is overcast with heavy black clouds and I can feel drops of rain and a cold breeze on my shaven head. My head feels so fresh and free. I feel so free. It is as if a heavy load has been lifted from my shoulders. We keep on walking in silence. I wonder if Skade can feel what I'm feeling. I can hear his uncoordinated footsteps trying to keep pace with mine but I am walking fast.

The rain starts falling heavily but I keep walking. My mind is transported back to my childhood when we enjoyed playing in the rain. We would sing, 'water us to grow!' We believed that rain would make us taller. Those games would end when an adult – any adult – appeared. In those days every adult person, whether you were related or not, was entitled to punish a child as his or her own. If someone did that these days, even if a parent is punishing his or her own child, it could lead to a few days spent behind bars. How things have changed since I was a child.

I hear the hymn, 'We are all visitors on this Earth', and I realise that I am getting closer to the Apostolic Church where Nosipho's funeral service is being held. I remember that I had vowed not to attend the funeral, Nosipho's funeral, my daughter's funeral.

'What's wrong?' Skade asks, noticing I have dropped my pace.

'I wanna go get a tie to put on,' I say, looking for an excuse to retrace my steps.

'C'mon man, what do you need a tie for? We are already here now,' he says, and I feel compelled not to turn back.

'Okay, let's go,' I say, trying to gather some strength.

The rain has stopped but I am so soaked that even my underwear is wet. As I enter the church doors I feel a cold wind running down my spine and my whole body begins to shiver. It is so strange that at the same time I feel perspiration on my forehead. Old man Jongilanga's voice echoes from the walls as he is having a heated conversation with the Creator.

'God, I call you teenage God because that's what you seem to be. Why do you dare take children and leave old wrecks like myself on this Earth? Are you the same God of Nazareth? The God who rescued the Israelites from Egypt. Are you the same God who with just a touch of the hand cured a man afflicted with leprosy? If so, your long record of experience should get rid of the abominations of this world . . .'

Probably hearing whispers from his audience, old man Jongilanga stops his confrontational prayer and looks in my direction. The rest of the congregation turns to look at me as if I have risen from the dead. I can hear people whispering, 'It's him', and others asking, 'What's he doing here?' They don't seem to care much about Skade who is standing next to me. I walk straight to the pulpit where old man Jongilanga is standing. He moves to the side and ushers me onto the podium. I hear some suggesting that I have sent my mind on a holiday and remained behind with an empty head. I wonder if they are right or wrong because I am not sure myself. Nevertheless, I have decided to voice what is inside me and others can decide whether it's driven by madness or not.

Water is dripping from the blazer I am wearing. I clear my throat and hesitantly greet the mourners. No one responds so I decide to go ahead with what I have to say.

'I am sure everybody is amazed that I am here today after having repeatedly refused to come and speak at this funeral . . .' I speak very slowly with constant pauses. I clear my throat again and continue, 'I am obviously embarrassed to stand and speak here today as everyone would expect. I refused to come and speak here because my relationship with Nosipho goes far beyond that of a teacher and a student. It is through my mistakes that Nosipho is lying in this coffin today . . .'

'Good Lord, this miserable fool is wasting our time. Just push him aside,' an angry woman, probably one of Nosipho's aunts, shouts from the far left corner.

'Hush, woman!' Old man Jongilanga comes to my rescue. 'Don't be so disrespectful!' he says scornfully. 'Give the man a chance to speak!'

'Thank you, old man. Now, as I was saying, eh . . .' I try to recall my last statement.

'Are there any men in this house? Why don't you beat the hell out of this human waste?' the woman interrupts again.

'This is God's house. Let us listen to what this son of God has to say,' old man Jongilanga interjects. At this point Skade pushes me aside and takes the podium. My heart starts beating heavily against my chest because I know that Skade is a man full of surprises when in front of an audience. He likes to display the militant character he always wanted to be known as. I am disillusioned because I think that Skade would pretend our act of reconciliation earlier this morning had never happened.

'People of Sekunjalo, many of you know about my disputes with Themba. I have quarrelled with him on numerous occasions and over a number of things. As a matter of fact, many people know us as foes.' Something in me says I must walk out of the church and forget about the whole thing. Skade glances at me and continues, 'But today, I am standing here to ask you to lend him your ears. Over the past while I have watched Themba trying to redeem himself by contributing positively to the well-being of our community. Now,

I serve with him in a task team that will present the grievances of the people of Sekunjalo to the Makana municipality council. Themba is the first person I spoke to this morning. He had the courage to visit me in my house while I was still in bed. We spoke about the tensions that exist between us, and for the first time in a long time, I realised that Themba is still the great human being I knew him to be when we were growing up. He has made mistakes, that we all know, but today he showed me that he is remorseful and I believe that he deserves forgiveness for all his misgivings. I ask you to listen to him and find it in your hearts to forgive him, as I have done.'

With that, Skade beckons me to take the podium again. Now I don't know whether I should respond to what Skade has just said or I should continue with what I was trying to say before his intervention.

'Further to what Skade has just said, I would like everyone to understand that I am a man. I am a human being. I have moments of joy; I also have moments of despair. I appear strong, but I am as soft as any other human being inside. I laugh most of the time; I cry sometimes.' I cannot make sense of what my mouth is saying but I keep talking just to get everything off my chest. Who knows, I might never get this opportunity again.

'We don't have time for this sorry sight,' the woman shouts again. But I realise that everyone, except the woman, is listening attentively to what I am saying.

'As I was saying, as a man I have mistakes just like any other human being. It is a pity that some mistakes are irreversible. I am here today to ask for your forgiveness for some of the mistakes I have made in the past.'

'Oh, poor thing,' I hear Nosipho's grandmother say. She is seated in the front row wearing her black mourning costume.

'Those mistakes include implanting a seed whose fruit I never nurtured. The fruit that has now withered before it could ripen.' I pause and look around me.

Everybody is looking at me with great attention. I feel the tears welling up in my eyes and I don't try to force them back.

'Nosipho is that fruit. I am Nosipho's father...' I can't continue talking any longer. There is a lump in my throat and I can't speak past it. I blink once and tears start rolling down my cheeks in torrents. Probably noticing that my knees are failing me and the embarrassment I am causing other men by crying in public, Skade and old man Jongilanga come to my rescue. Each one of them holds me by an arm and they usher me to an empty seat. I sit in the chair cupping my forehead in my hands. Someone starts the hymn, 'The Lord gives; the Lord takes away'.

I am sweating profusely and old man Jongilanga gives me his handkerchief to wipe the sweat away. Skade uses his jacket to fan some air for me. I feel resuscitated and tell them to go back to their respective positions.

'Are you sure, my son?' old man Jongilanga asks.

'I'm fine now, thanks,' I say, and I really feel okay.

'I'll take care of him, old man. You can go back and continue with the programme,' Skade assures him.

Old man Jongilanga holds his hand high, signalling for the singing to stop.

'Before I say the Grace, I want everyone to understand the significance of Themba's profound deed today. Some men find it inappropriate to say I am sorry; Themba just did. Some men find it difficult to express their emotions; Themba just did. Some men don't cry in public; Themba just did because he is a human being. With that, I believe that Themba's repentance is most sincere and for that he deserves forgiveness from all those who have begrudged him for his past deeds. Moreover, I believe that Nosipho's body will now rest in peace. For it was Nosipho's last wish that Themba should speak at this ceremony. He has gone beyond that and acknowledged her as a product of his own seed. Nosipho died without knowing who her real father was. Now we all know. And Nosipho will not be an angry ancestor.'

Old man Jongilanga says the Grace and the procession to the cemetery begins. As the father of the deceased I am one of the six pall-bearers. We walk slowly towards the hearse. Mabelana is standing impatiently next to the vehicle. I look at my fellow pall-bearers. They are singing and walking with ease. They don't seem to have any emotional burdens. I have been to many funerals before. I have carried several coffins before, but this one is different. It weighs heavily deep inside me and yet it is at the same time the lightest coffin I have ever held. It is almost like carrying an empty coffin. Is this what the disease did to my daughter? Reduced her to a bag of bones.

I never imagined myself carrying the corpse of my child. My children should be the ones to bury me as I did to my parents. We put the coffin effortlessly in the back of the hearse. The coffin is decorated with flowers. They will be buried together with the coffin in the lonesome grave. They will decompose as will Nosipho's remains. The maggots will feast on my daughter's remains. I can't bear the thought!

I watch Mabelana closing the back of his hearse with indecent haste. It is clear that he wants to get the job done and then move on to the next burial. To him it's business as usual. I don't want to see the coffin sinking down into the deep grave. I don't want to believe that my child lived fifteen years of her life without receiving fatherly love, or even knowing her real father. I don't want to go to the cemetery and hear people say, 'Soil unto soil; dust unto dust.'

I turn and walk away. I hear people asking, 'Where is he going?' But I ignore them and keep walking. I can hear torrents of abuse following me. I have done what I can to express my remorse to the community. Some might forgive me while others will not be able to look beyond my regrettable past. I hope that whatever questions Nosipho had during her lifetime have now been answered and that her soul will rest in peace. I don't care what happens to me now. Maybe this is how my life was supposed to end up. I was demoted from my job; I lost my position as a councillor; I was rejected by my family and then by the whole community. In fact, I am not needed on this Earth.

I know that when old man Jongilanga told me how I had survived abortion he meant to prove that I am strong. But now it makes better sense to me to acknowledge that I am an accidental creation, a product of careless conception. If the abortion had been successful many people would have been spared from the suffering that I have caused. Now it is time to end all of that suffering, I say to myself. But first, I decide to go and say a proper goodbye to my wife and remaining children. My soul will not rest in peace until I apologise to Thuli and our children. They may not readily accept my apology, but it will help me to be at peace with myself.

I walk boldly towards Aunt Nana's house. I know she resents me more than anything on the face of the Earth, but I'm going there anyway. I just want to see my family.

As I enter the gate her ferocious bulldog barks at me but I ignore it. A part of me is amazed by my courage. Normally I would not even come close to the yard. I knock at the door. I knock again.

'Okay, okay, I'm coming!' a rather hoarse and irritable voice says inside. I recognise it as Aunt Nana's voice. After a short while the doorknob turns and an unfriendly face appears on the other side of the half open door.

'What do you want?' she asks with undisguised contempt. She has one hand on the doorknob and the other on her hip.

'I . . . I would like to see the children, and Thuli. Thuli and the children . . . I would like to see . . .' I speak incoherently and my voice is shaking.

Her face frowns and she looks like she is about to vomit.

'Are they, are they in?' I ask.

'After what you have done you come just like that to say you want to see them? *Sies*, man!' She spits on the floor. 'Get out of my sight!' she adds as she is about to close the door on me.

'I just need to talk to them . . .' I try to explain the purpose of my visit.

'Thuli,' Aunt Nana interjects before I can say any more, 'get this miserable fool out of my yard.'

I turn and see Thuli behind me, holding a handbag and a Bible in her hands. She is wearing her pink dress. I like that dress on her. I asked her to put it on when we went to exchange marriage vows in front of the magistrate nine years ago. It's the kind of dress that turned men's heads as she went past; hence I preferred that she wore it only when I was with her. She was smaller then, but now she has a fuller figure and the dress exposes her curvaceous structure so vividly that I feel a certain kind of chemistry, as if I'm seeing her for the first time.

'Please let him in, Aunt Nana,' Thuli says in her usual ladylike and meticulous manner. I heave a sigh of relief as Thuli leads me into the house. I know the social worker in her will handle the situation with great skill even if we disagree. Aunt Nana disappears into her bedroom.

Oh, what a wonderful ex-wife I have, I think to myself as I stand in front of her. I feel even more sentimental than that fateful day when I was about to express my love to her for the first time at high school.

'Thuli, I've come to say I'm sorry . . .' Before I can say more my emotions fail me. I don't wipe away my tears. They stream down like waterfalls. I hold her left hand with both of my hands. She is still wearing her wedding ring. I heave another deep sigh and clear my throat. I let go of her hand so that I can wipe the tears that are streaming down my cheeks.

'I am sorry for being such a nuisance in your life. I know I have caused so much hurt and pain in your life, but I promise that you will hear no more of that after today. You will hear unpleasant news about what happened at Nosipho's funeral this morning. I am sorry about the embarrassment that the news will cause you. It's been eating me. I could not hide the truth any longer. Please forgive me, Thuli . . .' I am still not sure how to explain this to Thuli.

'I know about it all,' she says sternly.

'You do?' I ask with shock.

'Yes, I was at the funeral today. I was so proud when you admitted that Nosipho was your child. I had always wondered why Nozizwe looked so much like her. I was so proud that you said "I am sorry". The monster that I was married to could not have pronounced those words. And I was proud that you cried in front of many pairs of eyes staring at you. Crying is the expression of a true self. A man cannot cry unless there is pain imbedded deep down in his heart. That's why I am proud of you.'

She grabs my hand and draws me closer to her body. We embrace for a while and the warmth of her body and the scent of her perfume remind me of the closeness we have missed in these past few months.

'Thuli . . . I . . . I am sorry for having treated you the way that I did.' My voice is shaking and my nose is clogged, which makes my voice sound very strange in my ears. 'If there's anything I've learned from the time of our separation, it's to appreciate you, the wonderful woman that you are.' I feel her chest rising and falling as she begins to breathe heavily against my chest. 'Life isn't as pleasant without you. I miss you, Thuli.'

'I have missed you too, honey.' I suspect that I am hallucinating as I hear Thuli referring to me as 'honey'. That kind of vocabulary vanished in our marriage as we grew older. I feel like kissing her instantly.

'In fact, it's more than just missing you. I need you. Please forgive me, Thuli. I am prepared to do anything you want, just to have you back in my life. I want us to live as the family that we are.' By now I am crying openly, without even trying to hold back the tears. 'Please give me a second chance. I'll be a good husband to you, and a good father to our children. I promise. I'll do everything right this time. I'll be a good man . . .'

Thuli starts weeping as her face is buried against my chest. I squeeze her closer to my body. Aunt Nana walks in and finds us locked in a tight embrace.

'When a man cries a woman has to cry too,' I hear her mumble as she disappears back into her bedroom. We are still locked in each other's arms. No one says anything. Only tears roll down in torrents. Mine are not tears of sadness. They are not tears of joy either. They are the expression of the infinite longing for complete humanness. To be a man among men. To love and be loved. To be capable of feeling pain for myself and for others. To cry when hurt. That's what makes a man. Without tears he is incomplete.